K 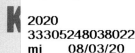 R BRADLEY

fighting words

 DIAL BOOKS FOR YOUNG READERS

DIAL BOOKS FOR YOUNG READERS

An imprint of Penguin Random House LLC, New York

Copyright © 2020 by Kimberly Brubaker Bradley

Penguin supports copyright. Copyright fuels creativity, encourages diverse voices, promotes free speech, and creates a vibrant culture. Thank you for buying an authorized edition of this book and for complying with copyright laws by not reproducing, scanning, or distributing any part of it in any form without permission. You are supporting writers and allowing Penguin to continue to publish books for every reader.

Dial & colophon is a registered trademark of Penguin Random House LLC

Visit us online at penguinrandomhouse.com

Library of Congress Cataloging-in-Publication Data is available

Printed in the United States of America
ISBN 9781984815682
Design by Jason Henry • Text set in Compatil Letter

1 3 5 7 9 10 8 6 4 2

This book is a work of fiction. Any references to historical events, real people, or real places are used fictitiously. Other names, characters, places, and events are products of the author's imagination, and any resemblance to actual events or places or persons, living or dead, is entirely coincidental.

For any child who needs this story:
You are never alone.

And for Bart
always

1

My new tattoo is covered by a Band-Aid, but halfway through recess, the Band-Aid falls off. I'm hanging my winter coat on the hook in our fourth-grade classroom when my teacher, Ms. Davonte, walks by and gasps.

"Della," she says, "is that a tattoo?"

I hold up my wrist to show it to her. "It's an ampersand," I say, careful to pronounce the word correctly.

"I know that," Ms. Davonte says. "Is it *real*?"

It's so real, it still hurts, and the skin around it is red and puffy. "Yes, ma'am," I say.

She shakes her head and mutters. I am not one of her favorite students. I may be one of her least favorites.

I don't care. I love, love, love my ampersand tattoo.

. . .

I am ten years old. I'm going to tell you the whole story. Some parts are hard, so I'll leave those for later. I'll start with the easy stuff.

My name is Delicious Nevaeh Roberts. Yeah, I know. With a first name like that, why don't I just go by Nevaeh? I never tell anyone my name is Delicious, but it's down in my school records, and teachers usually blurt it out on the first day.

I've had a lot of first days lately.

If I can get it in before the teacher says *Delicious* out loud, I'll say, "I go by Della." I mean, I'll say that anyhow— *I answer to Della, not Delicious, thank you*—but it's easier if no one ever hears *Delicious*.

Once a boy tried to lick me to see if I was delicious. I kicked him in the— Suki says I can't use bad words, not if I want anybody to read my story. Everybody I know uses bad words all the time, just not written down. Anyway, I kicked him right in the zipper of his blue jeans—let's say it like that—and it was me that got in trouble. It's always the girl that gets in trouble. It's usually me.

Suki didn't care. She said, *You stick up for yourself, Della. Don't you take crap from nobody.*

Can I say *crap* in a story?

Anyhow, she didn't say *crap*. She said something worse.

Lemme fix that. Suki says whenever I want to use a bad word, I can say *snow*. Or *snowflake*. Or *snowy*.

I kicked him right in the snow.

Don't you take snow from nobody.

Yeah, that works.

Okay, so back to me. Delicious Nevaeh Roberts. The Nevaeh is *heaven* spelled backwards, of course. There's usually at least one other girl in my class called Nevaeh. It's a real popular name around here. I don't know why. It sounds dumb to me. *Heaven* backwards? What was my mother thinking?

Probably she wasn't. That's just the truth. My mother is incarcerated. Her parental rights have been terminated. That just happened lately. Nobody bothered to before, even though by the time she gets out of prison, I'll be old enough to vote.

I can't remember her, except one tiny bit like a scene from a movie. Suki says she was no better than a hamster when it came to being a mother, and hamsters sometimes eat their babies. It was always Suki who took care of me. Mostly still is.

Suki's my sister. She's sixteen.

I'm still on the easy part of the story, if you can believe that.

Suki's full name is Suki Grace Roberts. Suki isn't short for anything, though it sounds like it should be. And that Roberts part—well, that's our mother's last name too. Suki and me, we don't know who our fathers are, except they were probably different people and neither one of them was Clifton, thank God. Suki swears that's true. I believe her.

Can you say *God* in a story? 'Cause I wasn't taking His name in vain, right there. I really am thanking God, whatever God there is, that Clifton ain't my daddy.

Suki used to have a photograph of Mama, from her trial. White pale face, sores on it, black teeth from the meth, pale white lanky hair. Suki says she bleached her hair, but whatever, you can see it's got no texture to it. Hangs like string. Suki's hair is soft and shiny, dark brown except when she dyes it black. It's a prettier version of Mama's hair, and her eyes look like Mama's too. My hair has bounce. It tangles up all the time. My eyes are lighter than Suki's and Mama's.

Suki's skin is skim-milk white, so pale, her belly almost looks blue. She burns bright red when she goes out in the sun. My skin's browner, and I don't never need sunscreen, no matter what Suki says. So while me and Suki don't know one single thing about our fathers, we're guessing they weren't the same.

Which is good, right? Because if the same guy stuck around long enough to be the daddy to both me and Suki, he should've stayed and helped us out of this mess. Otherwise he'd just be a snowman. What Suki thinks, and me too, is that Mama probably never told either of our daddies that she was going to have their baby, so we can't blame them for not being around. It's possible they were great guys, fantastic in just every way except of course for hanging out with our mother, who was always a hot mess.

Suki and me gave up on Mama a long time ago. Had to. Not only is she incarcerated, she had what's called a psychotic break as soon as she got to prison. It comes from the meth, and it means she's bad crazy in a permanent way. She wouldn't likely even recognize us were we to walk into her cell, not that we could, since she's incarcerated in Kansas somewhere, which we have no current means of getting to. She doesn't write or call because she can't write or call, not so as she would make any sense. And it would never occur to her to do so. She's forgotten all about us. I'm sorry about that, real sorry, but it's nothing I can change.

I got a big mouth. That's a good thing. It's excellent. Let me tell you a story to explain. Last week at school—this was a couple of days before I showed up with my new tattoo—Ms. Davonte told us we all had to draw family trees. She showed us what she wanted: lines drawn like branches, mother, father, grandparents. Aunts and uncles and cousins.

My tree would dead-end at Mama, behind bars, with Suki sticking off to one side. Wasn't no way I was going to draw that, especially since I suspected it was something Ms. Davonte planned to hang up in the hall outside our classroom for the entire school to see.

Ms. Davonte still doesn't get it. I don't know why not. I thought she was starting to.

Instead of a family tree, I drew a wolf. I'm getting better at wolves. I made her eyes dark and soft but her mouth open, showing fangs. I borrowed Nevaeh's silver markers to outline her fur.

Ms. Davonte came past and said, "Della, what are you doing? That's not the assignment."

I said, "This wolf *is* my family tree." I gave her a look.

Ms. Davonte doesn't know my whole story, but she knows an awful lot of it. Especially given all that's happened lately. If Ms. Davonte stopped to think, even for just a moment, I bet she maybe could guess why I didn't want to draw a family tree. Nope. She tightened her lips and said, "I want you to do the assignment I gave you."

I said, "The assignment is snow."

I got in trouble for saying *snow*.

I knew I would. It's why I said it. I got to take a little trip down to the principal's office. The principal and I are practically friends by now. Her name is Dr. Penny. (Penny is her last name. I asked.)

Dr. Penny said, "Della, to what do I owe the pleasure of seeing you this time?"

I said, "I'm not doing that assignment. I can't fix my family tree, and it's nobody's business but mine."

"Oh," said Dr. Penny. Then she asked what I was doing instead of the assignment, and then she agreed that drawing a wolf seemed like a reasonable compromise. She said she'd have a word with Ms. Davonte.

I said, "Luisa doesn't want to draw her family tree, either. Or Nevaeh." Nevaeh's dad left a few years ago. Luisa, I didn't know her whole story, but I saw the way her eyes emptied out when Ms. Davonte told us what she wanted us to do. "Ms. Davonte is still not listening until she has to."

Dr. Penny sighed. I don't know who she was sighing at. She said, "I'll talk to her, Della."

I said, "She ought to be paying better attention." I'm only ten years old, and I noticed Luisa's eyes and the way Nevaeh's shoulders tightened. Ms. Davonte is the *teacher*.

Francine says you can trust some people, but not all of them. I didn't think I would ever trust Ms. Davonte.

Dr. Penny said, "It might be helpful, Della, if you quit using words like *snow*."

I said, "Probably not." I wasn't trying to give her lip. I said, "When I said *snow* I got to come down here and explain this to you. If I didn't say *snow*, I'd have to say why I don't want to draw a family tree. The whole class would have heard my business. And then I'd get made fun of on the playground."

Dr. Penny paused. She looked at me for what felt like a long time. Then she said, "Thank you for that explanation." She suggested I sit in the comfy chair in her office until recess. She had a shelf of books I could read. I don't like books much, but there was one about dinosaur poop that was interesting.

I don't know what Dr. Penny said to Ms. Davonte, but I didn't have to make a family tree, and Ms. Davonte didn't hang any of them in the hall.

See? It's useful, having a big mouth. Next thing I'm gonna do with it is help put Clifton in prison for a long, long time.

We are still on the easy parts of the story.

2

Suki and I live with Francine. She's our foster mother. That's the word they use, foster *mother*, but there is nothing motherly about Francine. She don't even have meth for an excuse.

"Happy to have you," she said, when the social worker first brought us to her house. That was a couple of months ago, late August, still hot every single day. It was a week after we got away from Clifton. Feels like a year ago. A lifetime. But it wasn't.

Francine's house was half of a double-house, if you will, with a tiny little yard and a cramped living room. It wasn't dirty and it smelled okay. "Here's your bedroom," Francine said. "I don't usually take girls as young as you, Della, but I like that you two are sisters. Probably won't fight as much."

Back then Suki and I never fought with each other.

The bedroom was nice. Bunk bed made up with sheets and pillows and blankets. Two wooden chests of drawers. One each.

"Huh," Suki said. "Not much space." She took the plastic grocery bag out of my hand and dropped it into the top drawer of the first dresser. Dropped her own plastic bag into the top drawer of the second.

That was all the stuff we had. We were in a hurry when we left Clifton's place.

We were *running*.

"Beats the emergency placement witch," I said. I meant the woman who took us in the first few days. The room at Francine's was smaller than the one at the witch's house, but it seemed friendlier, and so did Francine.

Suki sniffed. "We'll see."

Back in the family room, Francine said, "Didn't they let you go back for your clothes? Books, toys, anything?"

"Clifton burned our stuff," Suki said. "That's what the cops said."

We'd seen the smoke from Teena's house. Clifton threw everything we had onto the burn pile in the backyard, doused it with gasoline, and lit a match. Cops said he was trying to pretend we didn't live with him.

Francine turned to the social worker, who was still shuffling papers. "They get a clothing allowance?"

Social worker checked her notes, and said we did.

So, soon as the social worker left, Francine piled us into her old junker car and drove us to Old Navy. I got to pick out whatever I wanted, *two hundred dollars' worth*. And Suki got two hundred fifty, 'cause she was older.

"Don't forget underwear," Francine said on the way there. "Socks, pajamas, whatever else. I ain't buying you anything more till your checks start coming in." She paused a moment. "You need school stuff? Backpacks, notebooks, pencils?"

I shook my head fast. No way was I spending my two hundred dollars on *that*.

Suki said, "Clifton wrecked my laptop. The one the school loaned me for the year."

Francine sighed. "I'll have to sort that out," she said. "I'll head over to the high school tomorrow morning, after I get Della settled. I work at the DMV, lucky they don't open until ten. You got a driver's license, Suki?"

Suki nodded. She'd taken driving at school and passed the test. She traced her finger along the passenger-side window. "Left it at Clifton's," she said.

"I can get you a replacement," Francine said. "We'll work on that too. You'll need to get insurance before you ever drive my car. You a decent driver?"

Suki said, "So far."

It was strange losing all our stuff at once. On the one hand, I loved getting all new things, and from Old Navy, no less. A fancy store. Most of my clothes came from the free clothes closet. Sometimes Teena gave me hand-me-downs, but since she usually got her clothes from the free clothes closet in the first place, they weren't actually any better. But I'd had a purple sweatshirt I really loved, and a couple of nice T-shirts.

I reached into the front seat and grabbed Suki's arm. "Hey," I said. "I'll be starting school wearing all new stuff." It'd be fabulous. Like I was one of the kids with a real mom who had a job and everything.

I was going to a new school. Not the one I'd gone to my whole life, and not the emergency placement school I'd gone to for the last few days. Brand-new. A do-over.

"Great," Suki said, not sounding like she meant it. She'd be wearing new clothes too, but to the same old place. Our town had a bunch of elementary schools, but only one middle school and one high school.

We went inside Old Navy and we both grabbed a cart. Suki walked with me to the girls' section. "Start with underwear," she said. She pulled out a seven-pack of hipsters, checked the size, and threw them into my cart.

"Hey!" I said. "Let me pick!" She'd grabbed white. I wanted colors.

"'Kay," Suki said. "Get what you want. One pair of pajamas. Two pairs of blue jeans and at least three shirts. Try things on. Make sure you've got room to grow."

I tried on blue jeans and found some I liked. Brand-new. I grabbed some T-shirts off the sale rack. Two hundred dollars was a lot of money, but Old Navy was expensive. Then I saw a hot-pink hoodie with OLD NAVY written on it in purple glitter. It wasn't on sale, and August wasn't exactly hoodie weather, but I loved wearing hoodies any time of year. All the fabric snug around my neck, and when I put the hood up, I could see people but they couldn't see me. Also I had *two hundred dollars.* I threw the hoodie into my cart.

I picked through the rack of shoes. I hated the shoes I was wearing but Old Navy didn't have much. I found a pair of plastic jellies my size. Six bucks, and at least nobody'd ever worn them before.

"Della!" I heard Suki call from another part of the store. "Get over here, quick!"

I hurried. Suki was standing in the center of the store, next to a table piled with shoes.

Not just any shoes. Purple velvet high-top sneakers.

Purple.

Velvet.

High-tops.

"Oh," I said. I'd never seen any shoes I wanted so much.

"Get them," said Suki. She was grinning.

"You too," I said.

"Nah." She waved her hand at me and laughed. "Look at the difference between your cart and mine."

Hers had blue jeans. Black underwear. Black socks. Black T-shirts and sports bras. Black eyeliner and mascara. If they'd sold black lipstick, Suki would have bought some. She liked black. Not me.

The purple velvet shoes cost thirty dollars, more even than the glitter hoodie. I put them in the very top of my cart and stroked them, just once. Me, tomorrow, first day of school: new blue jeans, glitter hoodie, purple velvet high-tops. For the first time in my life, I was going to look *fine*.

I'd added all the prices up so I knew I had enough money, but it turns out I forgot about sales tax, and in Tennessee that's a lot. My cart came to $221.

I thought about putting back the socks. The cheap T-shirts. But they didn't cost enough to make a difference.

I could get the plastic shoes.

Suki took the high-tops off the counter and put them into her own cart. "I'll buy them," she said.

"Really?"

She put one of her sports bras back, and a shirt. "You got a washer?" she asked Francine.

Francine nodded.

Suki said, "Then I'm good." She put her arm around me. "Gotta take care of my girl. Who needs more than two bras, anyway?"

I could always count on Suki. Suki fixed everything.

I put those velvet high-tops on my feet right there in the store. I was gonna throw my nasty shoes in the trash, but Suki said to keep 'em, you never knew when it might be handy to have a second pair of shoes. We went back to Francine's house and Francine ordered pizza for dinner.

Delivered. Pepperoni and sausage both. She opened cans of soda for us. Suki cut the tags off all our new clothes, and I sat and stared at Francine.

She was seriously one of the ugliest women I ever saw. She looked like one of those little dogs with mashed-up faces and pouches hanging from their jaws. Also she had little round bumps of skin sticking out from her face. I don't mean zits. They were zit-sized blobs that looked like they were on stalks, growing straight out from the surface of her skin. All over her face, and neck too. I started counting them. I got to thirty-six before she gave me the stink eye.

"Knock it off," she said. "They're called skin tags. They're not cancer, they're not contagious, and pulling them off hurts."

I said, "What if they *hatch*?"

She said, "If they do, it'll be into little monsters that attack you in your sleep and make you itch till kingdom come. So you better hope it doesn't happen."

When the pizza came, Francine slapped it on the table and passed out paper plates. "I keep foster kids for the money," she said.

I didn't mind her saying that. I liked to know where we stood.

"I only take girls," she said. "Mostly old enough to do their own thing. Two at a time, when I can." She stubbed her cigarette out on the edge of her plate. "I used to have a roommate, but it was snow, having to deal with people who never quite came up with their share of the bills. I thought, gimme roommates where the state pays their share, that'll be easier. Usually it is." She lit another cigarette. "Y'all going to court? Prosecuting?"

Suki nodded. She leaned over and slid a cigarette out of Francine's pack. Francine smacked her hand. "Nope," she said. "You're underage. I don't contribute to the delinquency of minors. Plus, trust me, you'd wish you'd never started. I do. So. You've got clothes and we'll figure out about the school laptop. What else you need?"

"Phones," Suki said. Clifton'd smashed hers. It was pretty new too. Clifton hadn't finished paying for it.

Francine shook her head. "Not my problem. You want one, get a job."

"Della's ten," Suki said. "She can't."

Francine shrugged. "She's ten. She don't need a phone. Neither do you. I got a landline in the family room. Use that."

"Seriously?" Suki looked annoyed.

I said, "We did too need Suki's phone."

Francine and Suki looked at me. Francine said, "Don't worry. You're safe here."

Suki laughed. "Yeah, *right*."

We threw the paper plates in the trash, and the pizza box, and that was the end of dinner. Francine turned on the TV and slumped in the recliner. Suki and I sat down on the couch.

"You see Teena today?" I asked Suki.

She grunted. "No. Quit asking."

"You had to," I said. "Unless she's sick or something." Teena was in Suki's grade.

"Didn't," Suki said.

Teena's mom had called the cops on us, which I didn't appreciate, but still. "Teena's our best friend," I explained to Francine. "She's, like, my other sister." I turned to Suki. "It wasn't her fault."

Suki jumped to her feet. "Bedtime."

"Suki," I said. "It's only—"

She grabbed my arm. *"Bed."*

"There's an alarm clock in your room," Francine said. "Get yourselves up however early you need. I'll drive you to school tomorrow, Della. After that you'll take a bus."

I put on my brand-new pajamas. I'd never had new pajamas before. They felt crinkly. "Brush your teeth," Suki said.

I rolled my eyes at her. I always brushed my teeth.

She said, "And get them tangles out of your hair."

I said, "You are not the boss of me." Which was a joke between us, because *of course* she was the boss of me.

When I came out of the bathroom, teeth brushed and hair as good as it was going to get, Suki was already under the blanket on the top bunk. I climbed up beside her and snuggled close. I said, "It's way too early for sleeping."

"Won't hurt you none," Suki said. She held her right hand up, fingers splayed. I put my left pinkie against her thumb and my left thumb against her pinkie. We walked our hands into the air, pinkie to thumb, pinkie to thumb, climbing up as high as we could reach. Suki'd taught me to do this and recite "The Itsy-Bitsy Spider," but we'd cut the spider song out long ago. When our hands were stretched as high as I could reach, we marched them back down.

"Skinna-ma-rink-y-dink-y-dink, skinna-ma-rink-y-do," Suki sang. "I love you."

I joined in.

Skinna-ma-rinky-dinky dink, skinna-ma-rinky do,
I love you.

I love you in the morning, and in the afternoon. I love you in the evening, underneath the moon.

Skinna-ma-rinky-dinky dink, skinna-ma-rinky-do.

I love you.

The car Teena's mother used to have had this thing called a tape player. It played music when you stuck little plastic cartridges called tapes inside it. Somewhere Teena's mom had picked up a tape with all these goofy kids' songs on it, and, since it was the only tape she had, she played it all the time. Teena's mom didn't drive us around much, but still, by the time that car quit running we knew every one of the songs, Suki, Teena, and me. Suki'd sung "Skinnamarinky" as my lullaby for almost as long as I could remember.

It wasn't even dark outside yet, but Suki'd pulled the curtains and the room was full of shadows. I tucked my head against my sister's shoulder. The bed was unfamiliar and my new pajamas itched, but Suki was the same as always.

That first night at Francine's, we fell asleep holding hands.

3

Suki didn't stay asleep. She thrashed around half the night, pounding on her pillow and flopping from front to back to front again. She must have woke me up a dozen times. Finally she settled, and we were both hard asleep when Francine's alarm clock went off across the room.

I jumped down but didn't know how to turn off the noise. I smacked some buttons. The numbers on the clock started flashing but the alarm kept going. I smacked some more. Nothing else happened.

Suki reached from behind me. She punched one button and the noise stopped. The clock went back to normal. "Figure it out, Della," she snapped.

"Good morning to you too." I loved it when she woke up like this.

In the kitchen Francine poured us bowls of raisin bran. She told us that it was the only kind of cereal she had in the house, and also that after this we'd be eating breakfast at school, because kids in foster care automatically get free school breakfast and lunch.

"You mean, like, hot lunch?" I asked.

We never got free lunch before, but Clifton usually didn't give us money for school lunch neither—or at least, if he did, Suki wasn't about to spend it on school lunch. We packed our lunches. Mostly peanut butter sandwiches. Sometimes chips.

Suki said, "I don't want to eat school lunch. Or breakfast."

"Suki!" I thought it might be interesting, eating at school. The school breakfasts always looked kind of tasty— muffins, juice, stuff like that.

"I always fixed Della lunch and breakfast," she told Francine. "I fed her. I don't see why you can't feed us."

Francine shrugged. "I'll feed you plenty. But if the state gives me a benefit, I ain't turning it down."

Suki stomped off to school, still muttering. Francine poured herself another cup of coffee. "You sure you don't need school supplies? We could quick stop at Walmart."

"Nah." Teachers always found a way to get me anything I really had to have. Most of the kids in my old school couldn't afford school supplies. The teachers were used to it.

In the car on the drive to school I asked, "So, foster mother. Does that mean you're, like, legally my mom?"

We had lawyers now, Suki and me.

Francine glanced at me. "It's kind of complicated. Clifton wasn't ever your legal anything—"

"Shoo," I said, "I knew that."

"And your mother should have lost her parental rights when she got sentenced to such a long prison term. But that never actually happened. The social workers are getting you and Suki named wards of the state. Until that goes through, I don't actually have much power."

She glanced at me again. "It doesn't matter," she added. "You'll be taken care of."

"I know," I said. "I have Suki."

"Suki can't have legal rights over you, though," Francine said. "She can't have legal rights over herself. She's only sixteen."

That didn't mean anything. Suki was still in charge of my world.

"How many foster kids have you had?" I asked.

"Six," she said.

"What happened to them?"

She didn't even blink. "None of your blessed business. Their stories are their own."

I thought for a moment. "Okay. What's your superpower?" Teena said everybody had at least one.

Francine tapped her hand against the steering wheel.

24

"I work with idiots all day every day and never lose my temper," she said. "Given some of my customers, not to mention my co-workers, that's a daily miracle." She took another sip of coffee. "What's yours?"

I said, "I don't take snow from anybody."

Francine snorted. Coffee flew out her nose. "Snow!" But she wasn't mad, she was laughing. "Grab me some of the paper napkins off the floor, there, will you?"

I did. Francine wiped the steering wheel. She tossed the dirty napkins back to the floor. "What's Suki's superpower?" she asked.

"She can make herself invisible," I said.

The school was big, brick, kind of shabby, just like my old one. The security officer smiled at me. The principal introduced herself—Dr. Penny—and shook my hand.

My new teacher, Ms. Davonte, didn't. She didn't even smile. She didn't look glad to see me at all. The first thing she said was, "I don't know where we're going to fit in another desk."

Like that was my fault. Everyone in the class stared at me. Nobody smiled. I said, "I can sit on the floor."

A boy in the front row, white skin, freckled face, plain brown hair, said, just loud enough for me to hear, "Next to the garbage can." The boys sitting near him snickered.

Ms. Davonte said, "Strike one, Trevor. And it's only eight o'clock." She walked over to the whiteboard and drew a slash under the name TREVOR written in the corner of the board. Trevor sighed, rolled his eyes, and muttered something else. Ms. Davonte said, "What was that?"

Trevor said, "Nothing."

Ms. Davonte said, *"What?"*

Trevor said, "Nothing. Ma'am."

Ms. Davonte turned back to me like she'd half forgotten I was there. She sent someone off to the custodian's to get another desk. She looked down at the papers the principal gave her, frowned, and looked back up at me.

I knew what she was thinking. I said, "I go by Della."

She nodded. "Good." She introduced me to the class as Della, not Delicious. She didn't make me say anything else, which I appreciated. The custodian brought in a desk. Ms. Davonte made everyone in Trevor's row, except Trevor, get up and push their desks back a space. She put me in between them and Trevor.

"How come I don't get to move back?" Trevor asked. "Put the new girl in the front."

"I don't think so," Ms. Davonte said.

Then she said she was just about to pass out a math quiz. She wouldn't expect me to do well, but she'd have me take it to see what I knew. She said, "Do you have a pencil, Della?"

I shook my head. Her eyes traveled from my face down to my glitter hoodie past my new blue jeans and purple high-tops, to my total lack of backpack or school supplies. When she looked me in the face again her expression had changed. Like, *Girl, maybe you should have got yourself a pencil along with those new shoes.*

I rolled my eyes and said, "My mama said the school had plenty of pencils I could use."

My mama never even put me into school—it was Clifton did that—let alone told me anything about pencils, ever, or cared if I had school supplies. But the whole class was still watching to see if I could hold my own, and I had to let them know I could. Like the way that boy Trevor made it clear he didn't care how many strikes Ms. Davonte gave him. You gotta be tough from the start.

4

Ms. Davonte found me a pencil. Said she wanted it back at the end of the day. Whatever. I went through the math quiz and wrote some numbers down. I didn't know any of the answers. Couldn't tell you whether I'd been taught any of it before or not. Sometimes stuff teachers say just doesn't stick. Like today—there wasn't room for math inside my head when it felt like the whole class was still staring at me. I had hoped my new shoes would help more.

Trevor turned around. "Nice shoes," he said.

I didn't know if he meant it. "Thanks."

He said, "Too bad you're so ugly, wearing them."

I guess not.

Ms. Davonte said, "Trevor, are you talking during a quiz?"

He said, "No, ma'am, the new girl asked me a question."

"Della," Ms. Davonte said, "please be quiet. If you have a question, raise your hand and ask me."

I raised my hand. Ms. Davonte nodded. I asked, "How come I have to sit behind this snowman?"

The class exploded with laughter. Ms. Davonte's face froze. When she got it unfroze, she said, "You're not getting off to a very good start, Della. We don't use language like that in my classroom."

Sure we did. I just had.

Ms. Davonte told us to pass our quizzes to the front. The girl next to me turned and whispered, "What'd you do that for?"

I nodded toward Trevor. "He's a jerk."

She said, "Ignore him. We all do."

I turned my quiz upside down before I passed it forward, but Trevor turned it right-side up when he took it from me. His eyes widened. "You're stupid!" he said.

Better stupid than a snowman. I was trying not to say that out loud, but I still might have, except that Ms. Davonte spoke first. "Trevor, that's *two*." She drew another slash under his name on the blackboard. "Three strikes and you don't get recess."

Trevor glared at me. "She didn't get in trouble for calling me a snowman—" More laughter. It's just hilarious, the word *snowman*. "Three." Ms. Davonte drew a third slash.

Since it wasn't even nine o'clock in the morning I wondered what she was going to threaten Trevor with for the rest of the day. I mean, three strikes is the limit, right?

Also, I felt bad. Because by rights one of those strikes should have been mine. I had called him a snowman right out loud, and hadn't gotten in trouble at all. That wasn't fair. The whole class knew it and I did too.

I took a deep breath and raised my hand. "Ms. Davonte—"

"Everyone in my classroom is responsible for his or her own behavior, Della," Ms. Davonte said. "I gave you a pass because you don't yet know our rules. Trevor, do I have to phone your mother? Again? It's only the third week of school."

Trevor scowled. Underneath the scowl I thought he looked afraid.

Ms. Davonte said, "Do I?"

Trevor said, "Nah." He put his arms on his desk and his head in his arms. He didn't move for the rest of the morning, not once.

The girl beside me whispered, "Only Trevor gets strikes. The rest of us just get yelled at."

I wanted to say something back to her, something friendly, but I didn't know what that might be. Also, shoo. I'd said enough for the first morning. I didn't want my name up on the whiteboard.

Suki had friends at school, but she never let them come to our house. The only friend I had was Teena. I had another once, for a while, back when I was small. June, her name was, but she went by Junebug. She was friendly and funny until the day I said "My mama cooks meth" when we were on the playground. Probably kindergarten, though I can't remember for sure.

"What's meth?" she asked, wrinkling her nose a little.

Junebug was black. She wore her hair in a dozen braids, with bright beads strung on each one. I loved those braids.

"You know, meth," I said. "It looks like sugar. Only it makes you act funny and sometimes it makes the room explode."

She nodded and we kept on playing, but the next morning she looked at me with big eyes and said her mama told her not to talk to me anymore. And she didn't. And when she stopped talking to me, a whole bunch of the other girls did too.

I asked Suki what did I do wrong. She said, "You can't tell people about the meth. Or about Mama or Clifton or any of this." She made a list of stuff I wasn't never supposed to talk about: Mama. Clifton. (*Especially not Clifton.* Not that he was gone most of every week, not that he wasn't our kin.) Meth. Prison. Who or what or where our daddies were. None of that.

I tried to win Junebug back. I sat next to her at lunch. I stood behind her in the bathroom line. I made silly faces. I poked her and I laughed a lot. Usually people like funny kids. Junebug ignored me for a couple of days. Then the teacher pulled me aside, told me quiet-like that Junebug's mama had called the school and asked them to make me stay away from Junebug.

I didn't have a mama who could call the school and stand up for me. And it's not like my mama could've hurt Junebug, not from prison, so I didn't understand why Junebug's mama cared. But she did.

Another time, couple years later, I got invited to a birthday party. A real invitation, printed out on paper. I brought it home from school. Suki said "No" but I really wanted to go, so I saved it for the weekend and asked Clifton.

"Sure you can," he said. It was Friday night, he'd just gotten home. He smiled, and I smiled back, happy even though Suki was shooting me stink eye.

The next morning I dressed up for the party. I told Clifton it was time to go. He said, "I ain't taking you, kiddo. I said you could go. But I ain't taking you there."

It was too far to walk. I went back to my room and cried. Suki got mad and said what did I expect and she hoped I knew better now. Next day the girl whose party it was asked me why I didn't show up. I said I wasn't interested in that kind of snow.

I was in that school for five years. I got myself a reputation early and it stayed.

5

Our first afternoon at Francine's, I took the school bus back to her house, like she told me to. Suki was already home, since the high school lets out first. She was in the bathroom redoing her eyeliner. "I'm going out to apply for jobs." She put down the eyeliner and studied herself in the mirror.

I said, "I'll watch TV."

"Nope," Suki said. "You're coming with me."

I started to argue but knew from the look on her face I wasn't never going to win. I settled for the promise that if I went with her all the way to the Food City down on the parkway, she'd buy me a slushie at Sonic on the way home.

"A small one," she said. "I've only got, like, five bucks. Maybe not even that."

She'd just come back from the movies when we ran from Clifton. Didn't have her purse, but she had the change from her movie ticket stuffed in her pocket.

Clifton's house was in a part of town where there was nothing but houses—old, crumbly, small ones, sitting off by themselves on patches of ugly grass. The city buses didn't bother going there, and it was too far to walk from there to anywhere else. To get to any sort of store, you had to take a car. Which meant, among other things, that Suki had never been able to get a job.

Clifton drove a long-haul semitrailer, so he was gone most of each week. He had an old beat-up car he kept out back for when he was home. In the last year or two, Suki sometimes borrowed it if we absolutely had to get somewhere, but she had to be careful not to use too much gas or let the neighbors see her driving. After she got her license, she sometimes borrowed Teena's mother's car, but Teena's mom charged her five bucks gas money, so Suki couldn't do that regular.

Francine's place was a lot closer than Clifton's to the center of town. You could walk one direction and get to the main street, or the other direction and get to a strip mall with a grocery store—Food City—and a lot of other things.

We headed toward the strip mall. Suki stopped at every single place that might possibly hire her. A dry cleaner's shop. A Putt-Putt. KFC. Each time, she made me wait outside, out of sight of the window. "I don't want no manager thinking I'll be dragging a kid along," she said.

"Then why drag me now?" I was plenty old enough to stay home alone. I'd done it for years.

Suki said, "We ain't taking chances."

"But we did—"

Suki said, "Not anymore."

We crossed a busy street. Suki applied at Lowe's and Long John Silver's and a place that sold video games. She applied at Dairy Queen. Little Caesar's Pizza. The grocery store, Food City. Then we walked home a different way and she filled out applications at Big Lots, Walgreens, another pizza place, and Sonic. After which she did buy me a slushie. Atomic Lemon. We sat on a bench outside the Sonic and shared it.

"How was school?" she asked.

I shrugged. "Fine."

"*Fine* fine or crummy-but-not-horrible fine?"

I grinned. "Crummy-but-not-horrible. The boy who sits in front of me doesn't like me."

"If you can, stay out of his way."

"That's what the girl who sits next to me said."

Suki nodded. "And if you can't, deck him. Don't you take—"

I said, "Snow from anybody."

The girl who sat next to me was named Nevaeh. Like my middle name. Ms. Davonte'd called her that. The girl hadn't spoken to me again, not once the whole day. At recess and lunch I'd kept to myself. Everybody let me.

I asked Suki, "What are we allowed to talk about now?"

She looked alarmed. "Why do you ask?"

"I mean—Clifton doesn't have to be a secret anymore. Does he?"

She shuddered. "I don't want to talk about him ever again."

If people had known Suki and me didn't really belong to Clifton, he wouldn't have been able to keep us. That's what he told us. We wouldn't have had anywhere to live. We wouldn't have had food to eat. We would have been out on the streets, which was not a nice place for two little girls, especially girls as pretty as Suki and as young as me.

Only: None of that turned out to be true. We *had* gotten away from Clifton and we *weren't* on the streets. Last week we'd had that emergency placement hag, and she was an old witch, but she gave us beds and meals. And now we had Francine, who was ugly but fine so far.

I sucked in a huge mouthful of slushie. It froze the roof of my mouth and my whole brain and gave me a headache all in a rush. I quick took a tiny second sip, just like Suki'd taught me. The headache melted away. I said, "We should have told on Clifton a long time ago."

Suki was watching the traffic on the busy road. She said, "Do not lay that on me."

Her voice rose. She'd gone from happy to ticked off in one second flat. I didn't have any idea why.

"I just mean—"

"Do you know what he used to threaten me with? 'Tell anyone,' he'd say, 'and you'll never see your little sister again.'"

"Snow, Suki—"

"You know that place on the way to your old school, off to the right, by the Lutheran church?"

"No—"

"It's a group home. For girls nobody will take into foster care. Clifton pointed it out to me every time we went past."

"Oh, yeah," I said, remembering. He'd say, "There it is, the prison for bad girls." Suki would always shrink a little when he said it, get smaller and quieter right in front of me.

Suki nodded. "He told me if anyone found out what we were doing, you'd go into foster care and I'd have to live in that group home. And then I'd never see you again."

Her voice could get totally flat sometimes, like a puddle of water, frozen.

"I called the place once," she went on. "I asked them who lived there. They said, 'Girls ages thirteen to eighteen who are unplaced in foster care.' So I knew that part was true."

"But the rest of it wasn't," I said. Clifton was a liar as well as a flaming snowman. We had evidence, after all. It was why he was still in jail. No bail.

Suki nodded.

"I'll make that video, and he'll stay in jail." Our lawyer told me they were going to videotape me telling exactly what happened, explaining exactly what the evidence showed. They'd show it in court when Clifton finally went to trial—it took forever for it to be his turn—so I wouldn't have to sit in front of him and say hard things in person while he glared at me.

Suki said, "Yep. Everyone knows what he did to you."

She didn't mean *everyone* everyone. It's not like we made the national news. Not like we were telling anyone at school. I wouldn't do that, not ever. Suki meant the cops and lawyers and caseworkers and such.

Suki shoved herself off the bench and started running down the road.

"Hey!" I ran after her. When I'd caught up, I grabbed her arm. "What's the matter?"

She yanked the slushie cup out of my hand and threw it into the street. The last bits of Atomic Lemon exploded across the pavement. A guy in a passing car honked his horn and shouted something rude.

"Hey," I said, but quieter.

She slowed to a fast walk. Her face was set hard, like stone, but tears rolled down her cheeks. "Suki?" I ran after her again, grabbed her hand. "We're okay now."

She looked at me. "You're okay," she said. "Sorry about your slushie."

I curled my pinkie finger around hers. "You paid for it."

I should have guessed, you know? I should have guessed the parts of the story that weren't about me. I should have guessed what had happened to Suki.

I've learned that some things are almost impossible to talk about because they're things no one wants to know.

Not even me.

That's the first hard thing I'm telling you. It might not look hard, not yet, but it's very nearly the hardest thing of all.

Sometimes you've got a story you need to find the courage to tell.

6

Francine was home when Suki and I got back. She said, "Next time you go somewhere, send me a text so I know where you are."

Suki shot her a dirty look. "With what, the landline?"

Francine laughed, as if Suki meant that to be funny. "Sorry," she said. "Leave me a note, then, will you? I ought to be keeping tabs on you."

"Soon as I get a job and a paycheck, I'm buying a phone," Suki said. "Then I'm getting one for Della."

Francine waved her hand. "Kid don't need a phone."

"She needs to be able to call me," Suki said. "If there's trouble."

"What kind of trouble she going to have?"

Suki said, "You been paying attention at all?"

Now Francine shot Suki a look. "She gets in trouble, they'll call me," she said. "That's what they do. I gotta spend too much of my vacation time hauling your snow-flakes outta trouble, y'all be living somewhere else. So maybe just don't get into trouble."

Suki said, "None of it was her fault. Snowflakes."

Francine said, "Wasn't her fault. Wasn't your fault, nei-ther. I'm not saying it was. I'm talking about whatever you might do next."

I might get in trouble, but if I do, it'll be Suki who gets me out. Always has been. Suki ran with me from trouble, took my hand and yanked me away from trouble.

I don't need anybody but Suki.

Suki said, "Maybe we can get her a government phone."

Government phones are free phones, for people who can't afford regular ones. No data and not many minutes, but they'll always work to call 911. Teena's mom had one once. It was better than nothing.

Francine rolled her eyes. "Nobody gives kids govern-ment phones. This lack of a cell phone thing, it ain't the tragedy you think it is."

"You could sign up for one," Suki said, "and let Della have it."

"How poor do you think I am?" Francine said. "I don't qualify for a government phone. I got a real job. I don't make minimum wage."

"That's right," Suki said, "'cause you're getting rich tak-

41

ing care of us." She'd looked it up online, at school. It was a boatload of money. Like, I can't believe the state of Tennessee gives anyone that much money just for housing Suki and me. We could live on our own with that much money, just fine. We would have.

"I get money for you *and* from my day job," Francine said.

"The minute I turn eighteen, we're out of here," said Suki. "Della and me both. I'll get custody of her and we'll live by ourselves."

"That's fine," Francine said. "You got, what? Eighteen months to go?"

Suki glared at her. "Seventeen months and three weeks."

Francine didn't seem offended. She just said, "It's all right. You'll get there."

When Francine said things like that, all calm and understanding, it felt like she was on our side. Teena's mom—I'd always thought she was on our side, but now I wasn't so sure. She called the cops when Suki begged her not to. She wouldn't let us just stay with her. And that emergency foster placement woman, the one the cops gave us to, she was nothing but nasty.

We were at the police station being interviewed. It was past midnight. I was so tired, I could barely keep my head on straight, even with Suki beside me tense and shaking. I asked could we go sleep in the jail. The policewoman said no, they had people on standby to take kids in, and someone was already on their way. She said it real nice, like we were going to get some sweet grandma type like you'd see on TV, who'd smile at us and tuck us in and maybe feed us cookies. Instead we got this worn-out white woman wearing too much makeup for that late at night, chewing breath mints, probably so she didn't smell like beer.

"This them?" she said. "Got any stuff?"

We shook our heads. We didn't even have Suki's purse. I wasn't even wearing shoes.

That lady—I forget her name 'cause I really don't care—she had kids and a husband and a nice little house, and they'd made over the garage into a kind of extra bedroom for emergency placement kids, with three twin beds and a crib, I guess in case they needed to take in babies in the middle of the night. (Who does that? Loses their babies in the night? Though Suki says our mama might have. It was just a matter of luck and timing.)

We curled up in one bed, Suki's arms around me, Suki's chin trembling against my head. I felt safer than at Clifton's, though that wasn't saying much. Suki and me have always slept tangled up together. We had two beds at Clifton's house too, but we only ever slept in one.

The next morning the emergency woman liked to have a fit when she saw Suki and me sharing a bed. She yammered on about how it wasn't right, like somehow we were using the bed for something other than sleeping in. She said, "I heard what kind of accusations y'all are making."

I didn't get what she meant, not right away. Suki's eyes flashed fire. She said, "Then you know my *little sister* needed someone to *protect* her."

Nasty woman said, "How do I know what's true?"

That was my first understanding that what happened to us was going to be hard to talk about not just because I didn't want to or really know how. It was going to be hard to talk about because people didn't want to hear it.

I hadn't said one word to the emergency woman, not a single word the whole night before. I said one now. "Snowman." Only it wasn't *snowman*, of course, and it may have rhymed with something you've gotta scratch.

So that didn't go well. She couldn't send us to school because I didn't have shoes, and she didn't want to spend money buying me shoes, but on the other hand couldn't exactly expect me to show up at school or later in court barefoot. Finally Suki said, "There's a free clothes closet downtown." Which you would have thought the woman would have known, but I guess when you've got your own house and nice cars and kids that eat designer cereal and get onto the school bus with fancy backpacks with their names printed on them, you don't have to wear clothes other people have thrown away.

Teena and her mom went to the free clothes closet every couple months—there's a limit to how often you can go—and they usually took me and Suki with them. The clothes closet is this big warehouse that smells like old socks, no windows, full of beat-up clothes like you'd expect, run by church people who say things like "Have a blessed day" while giving you pity looks. The church people dress nice. They don't never shop at the free clothes closet themselves.

Anyway, we told the emergency nasty foster woman where it was. She took us there, and I found an old pair of tennis shoes that completely creeped me out 'cause I hate wearing other people's shoes. Those were the shoes I hid as soon as I got my high-tops. Then I went along to the school, not my old school and not the one I go to now, some other school because it was supposed to keep me from feeling bad, somehow, about running away from Clifton, or who knows, maybe that woman just couldn't be bothered to drive me across town.

A whole new school for just three days and you can imagine how well that went. I was standing up front in yesterday's clothes and used shoes, and the teacher was looking like she couldn't believe she got stuck with a new kid half an hour before lunchtime on a Friday, and she said, "Here's our new girl—Delicious!" before I could get a word in. I said, "Call me Della," but nobody could hear me because they were laughing so hard. That's when the kid tried to lick me and I kicked him and the day kind of went downhill.

Francine is a big improvement, if you want the truth.

7

We ran from Clifton on a Thursday night. That means when I got to my new school, the Francine school, on Wednesday morning, it still hadn't been a week. Not even a full week with three schools, half a dozen policemen, two lawyers, two caseworkers, the emergency witch, and Francine.

The second day of school, Francine didn't drive me. I followed the kids off my bus into the thick August air, then into the cafeteria for breakfast. I was hungry, but I couldn't eat. The breakfast was chicken biscuits, cereal, fruit, and juice. A whole pile of food. I stared at my tray. My stomach rumbled. My mouth felt too tight to swallow.

"Hey," some kid next to me said, pointing to my biscuit. "You gonna eat that?"

I shook my head.

"Can I have it?"

I'd been thinking of wrapping it up in a napkin in case I felt better later. "Sure," I whispered.

"Thanks!" He ate it fast, three bites. I thought about asking his name, or telling him mine, but before I could say anything, he'd jumped off the bench and was gone.

Trevor got three strikes by ten a.m. It was an improvement over yesterday, but Ms. Davonte didn't seem to see it that way.

Trevor said, "It was the new girl's fault."

I said, "Nobody made you tie my shoelaces to your chair." Which he'd done. And I'd seen him do it, though he hadn't realized I had, so that the moment he started to get up from his chair, I yanked my foot sideways and the chair skidded out from under him and startled him so much he fell over. I yelled, "Who tied my shoes to your chair?" and that was strike three. No recess for Trevor.

Nevaeh, the girl sitting next to me, looked at me with her soft brown eyes. She whispered, "You could have just untied your shoes."

I said, "I don't take snow from anybody."

She nodded. I wish I knew what she was thinking. Sure couldn't tell.

At recess I talked to nobody. Again.

I took the bus home from school, and there was Suki dancing on the sidewalk, a smile on her face as wide as the sky. I got off the bus and she grabbed me and swung me around. "Food City called!" she said. "I got a job!"

"Great," Francine said, when she got home and heard the news. She popped us into her car and took us right back to Old Navy, because Suki had to have a pair of plain boring brown pants as part of her work uniform. They cost $21.94, counting tax. She was going to have to buy a Food City shirt too—$20. "No problem," Francine said, getting out her wallet.

Suki said, "I'll pay you back."

She was starting right away. They wanted her to go in for training on the long shift, Friday night, the very next day. Six p.m. until midnight. "They're short of help Friday nights," she said. "Most high school kids don't want to work then. I wrote on my application I always could."

Francine nodded. "We can make it work," she said. "Usually on Fridays I go out with my friends. There's a good band at O'Maillin's this week. Bluegrass. But I'll come pick you up at midnight. That's too late for you to walk home. Once I get the car insurance sorted, you can drive me instead."

Suki said, "What about Della?"

"What about me?" I asked.

"She can't stay by herself," Suki said.

"Sure I can," I said. "I'm ten."

"No way," Suki said.

"Yes, way. You did before—"

"And look what happened—"

"I'll keep the doors locked," I said.

Suki said, "On a Friday night."

I hadn't thought about that. Suki was right. I didn't want to be alone on a Friday night. Suki and me, we pretty much hated Fridays.

Francine sighed. "This is why I mostly don't take ten-year-olds," she said. "I don't even know any babysitters."

"BABYSITTERS?" Could you imagine, me and some thirteen-year-old being paid to watch me? That'd go well. "I'll go hang out with Teena," I said.

"*No*," said Suki.

There was a funny kind of stillness. Francine said, "They did the right thing."

Suki said "Yep" in a way that let me know she didn't believe that at all. "But anyway, Teena's got a new boyfriend."

"Oh, who?" I asked. Suki rolled her eyes and shook her head.

"She can come listen to the band with me," Francine said. "My friends won't mind."

"No way," I said. "Hang out in some skank bar with a bunch of old ladies?"

Suki sighed. "I guess she can come with me. Sit in the deli. They've got tables there." She looked at me. "Just behave. The whole night. Don't you dare get me in trouble."

"You're kidding me. Right?"

"Your choice," Suki said. "Come with me or go with Francine."

That's how I ended up at Food City for six hours on a Friday night.

8

Suki made me stand out on the sidewalk of Food City and count to a hundred before I followed her in, so no one would know we were together. I took the dollar she'd given me and bought a Coke at the deli, from a black woman behind the counter who gave me the stink eye. I was allowed to sit at a deli table while drinking a Coke I bought and paid for, so there was nothing she could say, but she looked like she wanted to say plenty. Don't know why. I was wearing my glitter hoodie again and my new blue jeans and purple velvet high-tops. I looked nice. Wasn't trashing up the place.

Suki'd given me a pen and one of her school notebooks, to draw in to pass the time. Drawing was Suki's thing, not mine. Francine had given me an old magazine with a princess on its cover. I didn't know whether princesses were Francine's thing. They sure weren't mine. I took the pen and drew a mustache and devil horns on the princess. I sipped my Coke. I needed it to last a long time.

The grocery store was loads busier than I thought it would be. Since Clifton almost always came back from long hauls on Friday nights, he saved grocery shopping for Saturdays. But just now at Food City there were people everywhere, all the checkout lanes going at once.

Then I saw her—the girl who sat next to me at school. Nevaeh. She was walking through the deli with someone who looked like her mom. I waved, and she came right over and slid into the seat across from me.

"Hey, Della," she said. "Whatcha doing?"

"Hey, Nevaeh," I said. I showed her the magazine.

"That's Princess Kate," she said.

"Not anymore," I said. I added bristly eyebrows and fangs. "My middle name's Nevaeh," I added.

Nevaeh made a face. She took the pen from me and blackened one of the princess's teeth. "My middle name's Joy. Like 'Heaven's Joy.'"

I thought about that. "More like 'Heaven's Yoj,'" I said. "Or maybe Yoj Heaven."

"Your name backwards would be Alled," she replied.

I said, "I guess. Alled Heaven? Heaven Alled?" I tried to think how to say *Delicious* backwards, but it was too complicated and also something Nevaeh didn't need to know.

"Heaven called," Nevaeh said. "They wanted me to tell you something."

Didn't sound good. "What's that?"

She grinned. "They give out free cookies at the deli." She got up and went over to the counter. I followed. The black woman handed her a chocolate chip cookie without saying a word.

I said, "I want one too."

The woman said, "How old are you?"

Her name tag read MAYBELLINE. Suki used to have mascara called that.

"Ten."

Maybelline said, "For the free cookie, you have to be *under* ten."

"I'm still nine," Nevaeh said. She took a bite of her cookie. She didn't offer to share.

I wouldn't, either, but I wished she would.

Maybelline sighed. She reached into the display counter, pulled out another chocolate chip cookie, and handed it to me. "Here. Where's your mother at?"

Nevaeh flicked her eyes toward her own mother, who was over in the produce section putting bananas into her cart.

"None of your business," I said.

Maybelline said, "Better not be."

Nevaeh and I went back to our table and finished the cookies. I gave her a swig of my Coke. "I like your hoodie," she said.

"Thanks," I said. "It's new."

She nodded. "It looks new."

On the one hand, I wanted to say *I am not usually someone who wears fancy things.* On the other hand, I didn't want to say *I got this new hoodie with my foster-kid clothing allowance after I had to leave all my old stuff behind.* So instead I pulled out the list Francine gave me. "I got shopping to do."

Nevaeh's eyes lit up. "You're shopping by yourself? That's cool. You can get whatever you want!"

"Yes and no," I say. "Francine is not stupid." She'd gone online and made a list of exactly what she wanted. She said we had to give her the receipt.

"Wonder Bread," Francine had said. "I like Wonder Bread. Don't buy me that cheap snow, and don't come home with no whole-grain nonsense neither."

Francine ate raisin bran for breakfast and Wonder Bread and bologna sandwiches for lunch, every day, with one of those little bags of Doritos chips. Cool Ranch.

Nevaeh said, "Who's Francine?"

"Lady I live with," I said. "Me and my sister."

Nevaeh nodded. She didn't ask questions, which I appreciated, so I added, "I like her place better than where we lived before. Want to help me shop?"

"Hey," Maybelline said as we walked past the counter, "little girl. Where's your mother?"

Maybe it was because she caught me off guard, or maybe I was just testing things out, now that Clifton was gone.

Maybe I wanted to know up front if Nevaeh was going to get run off like Junebug. "Incarcerated," I said.

Anyhow, that shut Maybelline up.

Nevaeh just snorted. I grinned at her, and we took off for the produce section, Francine's list flapping in my hand.

9

The trickiest part of shopping off Francine's list was figuring out exactly where everything was in the grocery store. The second-trickiest thing was figuring out what Francine actually meant. "Wonder Bread" sounds easy enough until you realize that there's classic white sandwich, small classic white sandwich, and giant white sandwich. Turns out plain classic white was the correct answer, which I guessed right based on how many sandwiches that sized loaf would make.

"Oscar Mayer bologna." Thick cut? Extra-thick cut? Chicken and pork? All beef? (All beef thick cut is the answer. I guessed all beef right, because honestly, who wants to eat chicken bologna? But I went with extra-thick because that was what I would have liked. Francine wasn't snotty about it, though. She just made notes so I'd get it right next time.)

"Fat-free vanilla-flavored coffee creamer." Got any idea how many kinds of coffee creamer there are? More than anybody needs in this world or the next. Full-fat sugar-free, fat-free full-sugar, all kinds of flavors. Nevaeh and I took turns picking up the weird ones—*thin mint cookie?*—and pretending to drink them. We got to laughing pretty hard.

"Sorry about your mom," Nevaeh said, when we finished laughing. "Incarcerated."

"Yeah," I said. "Me too."

"Do you get to see her?"

I shook my head. "She had a psychotic break. Plus, she's in, like, Kansas. Something like that. Far away." I tried to sound casual. Didn't need Nevaeh feeling sorry for me. "I don't really remember her. Just the last day. The last couple hours."

"What happened then?" Nevaeh asked.

I took a deep breath. Probably it was better I tell the whole story up front. I said, "She blew up a motel room."

"*What?*"

I held up one hand. "Truth."

"Where were you?"

"Sitting on the motel room bed. Watching cartoons with my sister."

Nevaeh's eyes got real big like she didn't know whether she ought to laugh or cry. I couldn't tell her. Finally she opened her mouth, and blurted out a very, very,

very bad word. Blizzard bad. A whole pile of snow.

For sure that was the only honest answer I knew.

"Will your mom care?" I asked.

"About what?"

"My mom."

Nevaeh said, "Why would she?"

"Some people do."

"Nah." Nevaeh paused a moment, then said, "But that's awful. I'm sorry."

I swallowed hard. "Thanks."

Nevaeh nodded.

"My sister says addiction is a disease," I said. "So does my caseworker. They say you can't fault a person for having a disease, for not knowing how to fight it and for being sick all the time. But you sure can fault them for blowing up a motel room with their two little girls inside."

"Shoo," said Nevaeh. "I'd say so."

My heart was beating fast. It slowed down after we messed with the creamers some more. *French toast swirl.* I am not making that up. I don't know why anyone would swirl toast. Let alone toast from another country. And how that's a creamer flavor is beyond me.

We hadn't finished Francine's list when Nevaeh's mother came and said it was time for them to go. "Bye, Alled," Nevaeh said. "Have fun drinking up that fat-free sugar-free non-dairy peppermint mocha creamer."

"Bye, Yoj," I said. "I'll bring you my leftovers Monday, for lunch."

"Extra-thick-cut bologna!" she shouted.

"Classic Wonder Bread!"

Nevaeh darted back to me. "My uncle's incarcerated," she said. "We love him anyhow."

I guess that might depend on exactly what he done.

Or maybe not.

Not, I suppose.

I abandoned the list and the grocery cart and found Suki. She was working a checkout line all by herself already. "Go away," she said, barely looking at me.

"What time is it?" I guessed maybe nine, ten.

Suki glanced up at a big clock on the wall I hadn't noticed. "It's seven thirty," she said. "Another four and a half hours to go."

"I got most of the groceries," I said.

"Well, put 'em back," she said. "Everything'll heat up and spoil. You can shop for groceries at eleven."

I dug out a corner of a refrigerated section and dumped all our cold food into it, where I could find it again later. The rest, the cereal and bananas and lettuce and stuff, I left in the cart. They weren't going to go bad. I wheeled the cart back to the deli. Somebody'd swiped my half-finished soda.

I stuck the cart in the corner and curled up in a booth. I was nearly asleep when someone poked me. I jumped. It was Maybelline.

"Who's that checkout girl you were talking to?" she asked.

"Next time, wake me up before you touch me," I said. "You're lucky I didn't punch you. I wasn't talking to no checkout girl."

"Better not be a next time," she said. "My deli is not a Holiday Inn. Also, don't you lie to me. I hate it when small children lie. She your babysitter? Working two jobs at once?"

"Course not," I said.

Maybelline frowned. "Like I said, I hate it when—"

"Okay!" I said. "She's my sister. But she's not babysitting. I just happen to be here. I like grocery stores."

Maybelline studied me.

I said, "Suki needs this job."

She said, "You like spending Friday night at a grocery store."

"Sure," I said. "Beats hanging out at O'Maillin's with Francine."

Maybelline flicked her eyes toward Suki. "How long she working till?"

"Midnight," I said.

She sighed, then tossed me a cleaning cloth. "If you're going to be here all night, be useful," she said. "Wipe down them tables for me."

I couldn't think of a reason not to. It was better than drawing mustaches on Princess Kate. I went from table to table, wiping away all the crumbs, including from under the salt and pepper shakers and off all the chairs.

I checked the clock. Quarter to nine. Not even halfway

through Suki's shift. I looked over at her, and her fingers were flying, grabbing all the groceries and running them across the scanner, punching in numbers for the fruit. She looked great.

I gave the cloth and bucket back to Maybelline. "Anything else?"

She looked me up and down. "You can refill the saltshakers."

That sounded kind of fun. Maybelline gave me a big ol' jug of salt and I went at it. You'd think pouring salt without spilling would take enough concentration to get my mind off things, but the truth is, salt's another thing that looks a lot like crystal meth.

Clifton must have been away driving his truck the night Mama blew up the motel room. Clifton never did meth. I didn't know how much he knew about Mama's habits or how much he cared. I didn't remember anything about how Mama and Clifton acted around each other. Five-year-olds don't remember stuff like that. Suki was eleven when the motel room blew up, so I suppose she remembers more of it, but I never asked and she never said.

Mama took us to meet some other guy—not Clifton, I never knew his name—at a motel across town. The man was cooking meth, or he and Mama were cooking meth—even Suki didn't know that part, I did ask that. But being in a motel room makes perfect sense. Meth blows up all the time. Not even the worst addicts are dumb enough to cook it where they live. I have no idea why Suki and me were there. Would have made a lot more sense to leave us at home. Probably the opportunity just came up sudden or something—I told you before, Mama had no more sense than a hamster.

She was a lot like a hamster, come to think of it. Up all night. She'd have run round and round on one of those little wheels if she had one. Meth messes with you in all kinds of ways.

Anyway, Mama and whoever were in the bathroom, cooking meth, and Suki and me were sitting on the far bed away from the bathroom door, on this ugly weird slippery orange bedspread, watching cartoons. Mickey Mouse. Suddenly Mama yelled something and ran out of the bathroom, and so did the other person, and then the whole bathroom blew up. Flames shot out right around Mama, like in the movies, but she didn't catch fire.

"Get out of here!" Mama yelled. Suki snatched me up. She had to carry me right past the blazing bathroom to get out of the room. The air was so hot it hurt. Mama drove this old pickup truck at the time, had it parked outside. The doors were locked, because *of course* you always lock up your truck outside the cheap motel where you're cooking meth. Suki dropped the tailgate, shoved me up into the bed, and climbed up after. The smoke alarm in the motel room started blaring, lights were coming on everywhere, and all sorts of people were yelling and scurrying around. The guy who'd been with Mama took off running. They never did find him. Meanwhile the room was still on fire, curtains catching now, so all around the window were these orange flames, like decorations. More smoke than you could believe.

Mama tried to open the truck door, but it was locked. The truck keys were still in the motel room, with the fire. Mama kept working the truck door, over and over, pulling on the handle and saying bad words. It was like she'd forgotten all about us and the fire and the meth, and could only think that if she wiggled something just right the door would spring free.

"I can't get into the truck!" she yelled.

Suki popped her head out of the truck bed and yelled, "That's because it's locked, you snowflake!"

Then the firefighters showed up, and right after that the cops. Mama got taken away in one car, handcuffed. Suki and me got taken away in another, holding hands.

I don't know what ever happened to the truck.

Later on, the same night of the fire—oh jeez, I'd forgotten this part. What a thing to remember in the middle of Food City—Clifton showed up at the police station and took Suki and me.

We were sitting side by side on hard plastic chairs. Still holding hands. A policewoman had gotten us sodas and kept trying to tell us everything would be fine, but with Suki so tense, she could hardly breathe, I didn't trust anything the policewoman said. The fire had scared me. The police room, all weird harsh lights, the way Suki's hair smelled like smoke and her eyes were so blank, that scared me too. I remembered it all in one scene, like a movie, just while I was sitting in the Food City deli, pouring salt.

I remembered Clifton coming in the door. He walked across the room straight to us, and he knelt down and looked Suki right in the eye. He said, "I told you I'd come get you."

It sounded like a threat. Even still, at the time I'd been glad—glad that we had somewhere to go, that we had someone to come get us. I didn't know about people like Francine.

Suki's T-shirt had princesses on it. Those ones from *Frozen*. She looked at Clifton, then down at Elsa and Anna, and then, for just a moment, she closed her eyes. Flinched, like somebody'd slapped her. And when she opened her eyes again, I could see she'd made a decision. "Yes, Daddy," she said. She stood up. Clifton put his arm around her, gave her half a hug. Nobody touched me. We went out of the police station, and from then on Mama was gone and we lived at Clifton's house.

Clifton told them he was our father. He didn't show proof—didn't have proof 'cause he isn't—but nobody at the police station much cared. He had a job and he wasn't on meth. He got us set up going regular to school— kindergarten for me, sixth grade for Suki—and after a while, the social services people figured we were all fine, and quit poking around.

That was a mistake. The lawyer we got now, who's supposed to stand up for Suki and me, she said it was awful that Clifton never had to prove nothing, that no one investigated him at all. She said the State of Tennessee dropped the ball but good.

She said she'd personally make sure they didn't drop it again.

Uh-huh. Because I fully believe everything all these government people tell me.

Back then, I wouldn't have thought Suki and me had it so bad. We had enough to eat. We didn't have to keep moving around. Clifton always paid the light bill and we had heat in the house and cable TV. Even after what almost happened to me, I wouldn't have thought it was so bad, not really.

I was wrong.

My mama blowing up a motel room and us probably never seeing her again, that's bad, but it's not even close to the worst. I'm getting there.

Just not yet. Can we have some happy in this story? I'm about done with sad for now.

"Hey, Maybelline!" someone bellowed behind me. "Whatcha doing, putting your grandkid to work?"

10

It was a short old white guy with a round bald head and round eyeglasses and eyebrows that looked like they were made out of fur. Like everyone else, he wore a shirt that said FOOD CITY. He had happy eyes.

"I'm filling saltshakers," I said.

"You on the payroll?"

"I'm helping," I said. "Paying back the cookie."

"Where's your mother?"

"What's the deal with people always asking about my mother?" I said. "Nobody ever wants to know where my father is."

"Okay," the guy said, "where's your father?"

I shrugged. "Never met him."

"Tony, it's okay," Maybelline said. "She's a friend of mine. She ain't bothering anybody. She's shopping, she just paused to help out."

Well, that was nice of her.

The guy thought for a moment, then stuck out his hand. "I'm Tony Kegley," he said. "Friday night manager. You finding everything you need here at Food City?"

I shook his hand. "I'm Della," I said. "I got most of my groceries"—I nodded toward my shopping cart in the corner—"but I'm having real trouble deciding what flavor creamer to buy."

Tony's face crinkled like I'd made the best joke ever. "Don't go with creamer," he said. "Lord alone knows what's in that stuff. You want to water down your coffee, stick with good old-fashioned half-and-half." He nodded at Maybelline. "Looks like she's working harder than a cookie. Let her have something else to eat." He walked off, and I heard him saying to someone else, "Hey! You finding everything you need here at Food City?"

"He's nice," I said.

Maybelline said, "He might be the nicest man in the world." She gestured to the deli. "What do you want?"

I looked at the luncheon meat, the cheese, the cakes and cookies and cupcakes. Sushi. Who in their right mind would eat sushi? Especially sushi made at a Food City in East Tennessee. Fried chicken, meat loaf. Then I saw it. I grinned. I said, "I'll take some of that mac 'n' cheese."

It got late. I went around the deli and turned all the chairs upside down on the tables, so the night janitors could mop the floor. Maybelline said they'd do that once the store was closed. Maybelline started pulling the hot stuff off the deli line. I took my cart over to where I'd hid our cold stuff, put it back in, and took it over to Suki.

In addition to her paycheck for working at Food City, Suki got 10 percent off anything she bought there. That was why we were doing all Francine's shopping. Francine said, so long as we bought everything she wanted us to get, we could take the 10 percent and use it to buy whatever else we wanted.

Anything in the whole store.

Francine's list came to $147, which meant Suki got $14.70 off, which meant $7.35 for each of us. Suki took a quick bathroom break. On her way back, she went over to the cheese counter and picked out some weird mushy cheese with garlic in it. "Always wanted to try this," she said. It cost $6.99, so you can see why she never did.

I decided on Flamin' Hot Crunchy Cheetos, a family-sized bag, and a two-liter of Mountain Dew. Next morning, Suki slept in, Francine slept in, and I ate the whole bag of Cheetos for breakfast, washed down with Mountain Dew.

It was heaven. Or, you know, Nevaeh.

11

Monday morning, Ms. Davonte handed back the math quiz we'd taken on my first day. I got an 8. As in, percent. Eight percent. I'd gotten two answers right out of twenty-five.

Ms. Davonte said, "Don't worry about it, Della." Then she made me stay in at recess and go over it with her. She said my old school must not have gotten to this stuff yet.

They had, but I wasn't going to tell her that. She'd figure out eventually that school and me didn't get along. School was just a place I had to go.

I missed the entire recess. The school had a dirt playground with some big trees and swings and slides and stuff to climb. Instead of swings and trees and sunlight, I got extra math. The whole afternoon I felt twitchy. I tapped my feet under my desk until Ms. Davonte made me stop.

Someone knocked on the classroom door. Ms. Davonte answered it. "A note for you, Della," she said, handing me a paper.

It said I was supposed to take a different bus after school, not home, but to the after-school program at the Y. The note was signed *Francine*.

Not Suki. Francine.

Over the weekend Suki and Francine had been talking about some kind of after-school program, but I hadn't really listened. I never thought they'd spring it on me like this.

Plus I'd never gotten a note in the middle of school before. Plus I'd never been to the Y. I didn't really know what a Y was.

I raised my hand. "Is this real?"

"Is what real?" asked Ms. Davonte.

"This—" I held up the note. "It says I have to take the bus to after-school at the Y."

Ms. Davonte looked impatient. "Of course it's real. Why wouldn't it be?"

Nevaeh tapped my desk. "I go to the Y after school," she said. "It's real."

Okay, that much was good. But why was I even going? I could stay home by myself after school. Or with Suki, like I was supposed to.

By the time I figured out which bus went to the after-school program, it was almost entirely full. I could see Nevaeh in the way back, but there weren't any empty seats near her. I don't think she noticed me. Trevor was sitting in the very first seat. I went past him and squeezed in next to some little kids.

When we pulled up at the Y, there were buses from all the elementary schools, and a whole swarm of kids heading into the building. I didn't know what I was supposed to do. I stood around until a girl Suki's age pointed me to the front desk. I showed the woman there my note from school.

"You're all set," she said. "Head into the big room for snacks and homework time. Then it's either the gym or the pool. Did you bring your swimsuit?"

"No." I'd never owned a swimsuit.

"Bring it with you tomorrow," she said.

I'd never been in a pool. I didn't know how to swim.

She said, "Today you can play in the gym. Do you like wall climbing? Basketball?"

How would I know?

In the big room everyone was sitting down at round tables, eating granola bars. I hesitated in the doorway.

"Della!" Nevaeh said, waving. "Over here!"

I sat down at the empty spot at her table. She introduced me to the other girls. One of them, Luisa, was in Ms. Davonte's class with us. She had dark skin and hair, a thin face, big glasses, and a quick smile. I didn't recognize the others.

I sat and ate a granola bar, and then the teenagers who

were bossing all of us said it was homework time.

The only homework I had was redoing the answers I missed on the math quiz. That meant Nevaeh and all the other girls were going to see my quiz with the 8 written on top.

I took the quiz out of the folder Ms. Davonte gave me. I folded back the top of it to hide the 8, but I couldn't hide the red marks covering all the rest. I hunched my arms around the paper.

"Hey." Someone tapped my shoulder. Nevaeh. "Can I see?"

When I didn't move, she added, "I'm good at math."

I said, "Lucky for you."

The other girls looked at me like I was being snotty, and who knows, maybe I was.

Nevaeh yanked the quiz out of my hands. She actually did. "Don't—" I said, but she was already looking at it. She studied it for what felt like a long time. Meanwhile my face got hotter and hotter. I stared at my hands.

She looked up. "You aren't making careless mistakes," she said. "You're getting the answers wrong in the same way every single time." I didn't understand. "It's like if someone taught you that two plus two equaled six," she continued. "Every time you were asked to add two and two you'd put down six, and it would always be wrong. Here," she said, "let me show you."

"I don't want you to show me," I said. "I didn't want you to even look at it."

"But I can explain it to you," Nevaeh said. "Then you'll understand." She frowned. "I'm trying to help."

As if it was going to be any easier listening to Nevaeh than it had been listening to Ms. Davonte. I grabbed my quiz back, crushed it into a ball, and threw it toward the trash can in the corner of the room. I missed.

Luisa whistled soft between her teeth.

Nevaeh walked over to the trash can, picked up the crumpled quiz, and brought it back. She smoothed the paper flat again. "I'm sorry," she said quietly. "I was trying to help. I wasn't trying to embarrass you."

I didn't say anything. Didn't know what to say. Part of me wanted to rip that quiz to pieces and throw them all into the air—I'd like to see Nevaeh try to fix *that*—and part of me wanted to quit being such a snot.

I don't know which part would have won, because the counselors said it was time for recreation.

"Did you bring your swimsuit?" Nevaeh asked, sliding the quiz back without looking at it again.

I shook my head.

"Bring it tomorrow. Swimming's fun."

"Sure," I said. "If I remember." Would I be at the Y tomorrow? Was this an everyday thing? I wished I'd paid better attention to Suki and Francine. At least then I'd know more about what was going on.

Nevaeh and the rest of our table went off to the pool. I followed some kids I didn't know into the gym. It was huge—three or four times as big as the gym at my school.

A bunch of high school kids were already shooting bas-ketballs at a net in the corner. The after-school counselors divided us up into different groups—volleyball, Hula-Hoops, something with rackets.

"Ever played basketball?" one of the counselors asked me. "We play a lot of basketball here."

She was bouncing a basketball on the floor while she talked. Suddenly she grabbed it and threw it hard against the floor. The ball bounced once and hit me in the gut. It ricocheted off me and knocked into—oh, snow. Trevor. The strike-out king. He scowled and flung the ball back at me like I'd hit him on purpose.

"Cool it, Trevor," the counselor said. "It was an accident."

"Does he get strikes here too?" I asked.

"NO," said Trevor.

The counselor ignored him. "Sorry about that pass, I should have warned you. It's called a bounce pass. You ever played?"

I shook my head. We messed around with basketballs sometimes in gym at school, but that was all.

"Want to?" she asked.

I shrugged.

She showed me how to dribble, and told me to practice walking and dribbling at the same time. "Try not to look at the ball," she said.

She went away to help someone else. I dribbled. It wasn't very fun.

I made it halfway across the floor when I saw sneakers

in front of me. I looked up, and there was Trevor again.

He said, "Hey, stupid. You hit me with the ball."

I said, "Did not. Jerkface."

He said, "You're in my way." He grabbed the basketball out of my hands and hurled it across the gym. It rolled into the middle of the high schoolers' game.

One of them scooped it up. "Whose ball?"

I raised my hand. She threw it toward me. I tried to catch it. I missed.

Trevor laughed.

I went after the ball and chucked it at his head.

He ducked. The ball smacked into a white-haired man who had just walked into the gym. He was wearing shorts and a T-shirt, but he looked familiar. "Hey, sunshine!" he said.

Trevor was beaming at him. "Coach!" he said.

The coach shook Trevor's hand. Then he smiled at me. "We haven't met here before, have we? I bet you know me from Food City."

"Tony," I said. The Friday night manager. Suki's boss.

His grin widened. "Grocery store manager by night, middle school basketball coach by day. You working on your skills? Gonna be on my team next year? I coach both the girls and the boys."

Trevor'd grabbed my ball and was dribbling it. Coach held out his hands, and Trevor snapped the ball into them. "Come on—" Coach Tony looked like he was trying to remember my name.

"Della," I said.

"Della. We'll get a group together, run through a couple of drills. I come here after school until the middle school practices start. Keep my players sharp."

I looked at Trevor, grinning up at Tony like a puppy dog. I looked around the room. Looked at the basketball. I shook my head. "Not today."

Clifton never hit me, or kicked me. Sometimes he gave me what he called a snakebite. He'd grab my arm with both of his hands, and twist one hand up and the other down, so that my skin burned. It hurt, but it didn't leave a bruise.

Mostly what Clifton did was laugh at me. "You're sure big and ugly," he'd say. "Clumsy too." Or "Not good at anything, are you?" Or "Look at you run. Like a buffalo. Not much like Suki, are you?"

I was as much like Suki as I could manage to be. Which wasn't much. Wasn't enough.

Francine picked me up from the Y on her way home from work. When we got to her house, there was a strange car in the driveway. I ignored it. I was counting down the number of seconds until I saw Suki, until I could ask her just why exactly I had to go to the Y. I ran up the steps into the house. Our social worker was sitting next to Suki on the couch. I stopped dead. Francine bumped into my back. "Did you forget?" she asked. "You've got a meeting about your Permanency Plan."

12

Every kid in foster care has to have a Permanency Plan. It's a written-down goal we're supposed to be moving toward. Like getting back with your parents or getting adopted.

Problem is, nobody knew quite what to plan for Suki and me. We don't have family outside of Mama. Nobody's likely to adopt us, a ten-year-old and a sixteen-year-old, not that I'd want them to. Shoo.

Our caseworker wanted us to look on the bright side. Wanted us to think big thoughts about our futures. Wanted us to be people other than who we are. She said something about going to college, and I thought, *Have you seen my math quiz?* And Suki—her grades are worse than mine.

She's in remedial everything. Plus, who goes to college? Not kids like us.

"I turn eighteen in a year and a half," Suki said. "As soon as I do, I'm leaving foster care. I'll take custody of Della. We won't be your problem anymore." She tapped her fingers on the table. "That's our plan."

The caseworker put on her patient face. She was always doing that. I don't know if she couldn't tell that her patient face made Suki angry, or if she got patient on purpose to tick Suki off. It was one of the reasons I didn't trust her.

"What about *my* plan?" I asked.

The caseworker ignored me. "Where will you live?" she asked Suki. "Where will you work? You can't get custody of Della until you're in a stable situation."

"I've already got a job," Suki said. "I'm going to get a car and then an apartment. I'll save up."

"Good for you, finding a job already," the caseworker said. "That's super. How many hours a week are they giving you?"

"I just started last Friday," Suki said. "They said around twelve hours a week. But I'm going to try to get more."

The caseworker nodded. "At your age, when school's in session, they can't give you more than eighteen. You can work full-time in the summer. It's minimum wage?" Suki nodded. The caseworker scribbled on a piece of paper. "Okay. What are you responsible for paying for right now?"

Suki glanced at Francine. "I owe Francine some money. For my work uniform. And half the car insurance, when the bill comes."

Francine said, "I just put her on my plan so she could drive my car. I told her I'd pay half."

"That's very generous," the social worker said. She looked at Suki. "She doesn't have to do that."

"Cuts into her profits," Suki said.

The caseworker pursed her lips. "People don't take foster kids for the money," she said.

"Sure they do," I said. "She said so."

The caseworker and Francine exchanged a glance and I saw them decide to ignore me again.

Suki said, "I'm going to buy a phone, and then I'm going to get Della a phone. Then I'll save for a car. Then I'll save up for the apartment and stuff. That's our plan. You can write it all down."

"What about *my* plan?" I said again.

The social worker scribbled some numbers. "How much will the phones cost, each month? How much for the car insurance?"

Suki told her. "One fifty for the car insurance. But that's for the whole year."

"Uh, no," said Francine. "It isn't. That's per month."

"*What?*" said Suki.

"I'm sorry," Francine said. "I thought you understood."

One dollar and fifty cents didn't sound like that much to me, but then Suki said, *"A hundred and fifty dollars a month?"*

"Three hundred, when you count the part I'm paying," Francine said. "That's what car insurance costs for an inexperienced sixteen-year-old girl not related to me."

"Shoo," Suki said, her shoulders slumping. "I gotta pay that every month?"

Francine said, "If you want to drive my car."

Wow. I mean, of course Suki wanted to be able to drive. It would be useful, especially on weekends. And she'd have to have insurance if she got a car of her own. But that was a big chunk of change.

"So," the social worker said. "Let's look at the feasibility of what you're saying."

"What's that mean?" I asked.

"Your budget," the caseworker said. She took out another piece of paper and started a list. "Right now, let's say you're getting minimum wage for fifty hours a month. Minus two cell phones and half your car insurance. You might be able to save a hundred dollars a month, if you're careful."

"I am," Suki said. "And that's sixteen months, so—"

"Sixteen hundred dollars," the social worker said. "You might get more hours in the summer. Let's say you save two thousand dollars. If you work hard. If you really try to save."

I took a deep breath. That was okay. It was a lot of money.

"To get your own place, and custody of Della," she said, "you'll need first and last months' rent. Probably a security deposit. Rent's cheap around here—you might be able to find a two-bedroom for six hundred a month—"

"We don't need two bedrooms—"

"To get custody of her you do. Say $550 at the cheapest. So there's at least $1650 to get into a place. An electric deposit—that's likely a couple hundred dollars. Money for the first electric bill. Water, sewer. That's not counting anything like buying a car." The caseworker shook her head. "You're going to need more than two thousand dollars. And once you get a place, you're going to need to make enough to stay there. Minimum wage, even full-time, isn't enough."

"What about public housing?" Suki asked. "Teena's mom gets Section 8."

"You might qualify," the caseworker said, "but right now, the waiting list for those is two years long."

"Can I get on the list right now?"

The woman shook her head. "Not until you're eighteen." She said, "Look, Suki, I'm not here to rain on your parade."

"Sounds like it," said Suki.

"We have some special programs. If you were saving for a car, or a rent deposit, in some cases the state can provide matching funds. So if you saved a thousand dollars, we'd give you another thousand."

Suki blinked. "You're kidding."

"It's part of our Independent Living program."

I took a deep breath. "WHAT ABOUT *MY* PLAN?"

They all stopped and stared at me like this was the first time I'd said it.

"Jeez, Della, calm down," Suki said. "This plan is all about you."

"Well, you're not talking to me," I said. "You're talking to *her*. And you stuck me at the Y without asking me. Without even *telling* me—"

"I did not," Suki said. "I told you about it yesterday. Only we didn't know if they'd be able to take you right away."

"You didn't tell me! Francine didn't! And nobody asked if I wanted to go in the first place!"

"What do you want, Della?" Suki snarled. "I can't watch you all the time *and* work *and* try to save all this money. I can't keep doing everything for you right this minute and still take care of you once I'm eighteen. I can't! What do you expect? I've been stuck taking care of you since you were born!"

I sat back. Never. I mean, never. Suki worried and she laughed and she sang. She held my hand and she washed my clothes and she kissed me good-night. She never acted like she didn't want me around. Plus I knew how to do all sorts of things. I always helped.

"It's too much," Suki said. "Too. Much. Okay?"

Francine blew out her breath. "Sorry we dropped the Y on you like that, Della. We should have given you more warning. But I did think you understood."

"I don't want to go there."

"Tough," Suki said. "You are."

"Suki—"

"I can't keep doing everything," Suki said.

The social worker was just sort of staring at us, like we'd gone totally off topic and could we all go back to discussing her programs now? Francine said, "We need some mental health evaluations on these two."

It took me a second to realize she meant Suki and me. It took Suki less time. She jumped up from the table. "So now I'm CRAZY?" She bolted into our bedroom and slammed the door.

13

The social worker took a deep breath. "Looks like normal sibling conflict to me."

"They been through a lot," Francine said.

"We'll keep an eye on them," the social worker said. She looked at me. "Just the one time, right?"

I was sick of people asking that question. I nodded.

"So," the social worker said, "I think they should be fine."

Francine said, "There are a lot of ways to be traumatized. Their mother—"

I didn't want to talk about Mama. "She was a hamster," I said. Hamsters weren't traumatic.

The social worker made some notes. "I'll put in a

request," she said to Francine. She looked at me. "You don't want to be part of your sister's plan? You'd rather she not get custody of you?"

That wasn't what I meant at all. "Of course not," I said. "I mean, of course. I mean, I have to stay with Suki."

The social worker closed her folder. "It's a lot to process," she said. "I'll come back in a few weeks. Meanwhile, encourage your sister to stay in school. She ought to at least graduate high school. Plus"—her eyes softened, just for a moment—"if she stays in custody, she'd get a chance to be a teenager. She'd have some time to have fun."

Fun. Fun was Suki and me and Teena, watching game shows all summer morning, sprawled across our living room floor. Fun was the three of us at the carnival that set up every April in the high school parking lot. I ate a whole cotton candy once and then barfed hot pink on the Tilt-A-Whirl. The guy running the ride was furious and Suki and Teena laughed until they cried. We ran off, leaving him with the mess, and they bought me a second cotton candy since I'd wasted the first one.

Fun was the Monday afternoon feeling, when Clifton was gonna be gone for five whole days.

But here it was a Monday afternoon, and it felt more like a Friday to me.

When the social worker left, Francine went to our bedroom and wrenched the door open. "Slam it shut like that again, and I'll take this door off its hinges," she said. "Don't try me. I've done it before." I heard Suki growl. Francine came back into the kitchen.

"Why'd you say we were crazy?" I asked her. I was doing everything I could to act normal, all the time.

"I didn't say you were crazy," Francine said. "I said you were having a hard time. You need help, you and Suki. Nothing wrong with that."

I didn't need help. But apparently Suki did. Help taking care of me.

At dinner Suki tried to make nice. "You know I didn't mean what I said," she told me. "Right?"

I didn't say anything. Suki always meant what she said.

She smiled big. "What'd you do at the Y?"

"Nothing," I said. "Nothing fun. Can I come home and be with you tomorrow?"

She shook her head. "I'm working," she said. "Right after school. That's why we signed you up for the Y in the first place."

I could go with. I could hang out in the deli. "I was useful at Food City," I said. When she didn't respond, I added, "I'm useful all the time." I did do all sorts of work around Clifton's house. I knew how to vacuum and dust and put the dishes away. I helped cook sometimes. I could make sandwiches and cereal.

Suki still didn't say anything. She didn't even look at me.

"Your boss works at the Y," I told her. "Tony, the night

manager? He coaches basketball. I'ma tell him how mean you are."

She shot back, "As long as I do my job, I'm pretty sure he won't care."

That night, when we got to bed, Suki started singing just like always. *Skinnamarinky, dinky, dink, skinnamarinky do.* I didn't join in. "C'mon, Della," she said, hugging me a little. "Sing the night song with me."

I didn't. Didn't want to.

She went through the whole song a second time. Then she studied my face up close. "I hope you don't think we should have stayed at Clifton's."

"No," I said. "I never once thought that."

"Good," she said. She rolled over and set her shoulder against mine. In a few minutes she was sound asleep.

A couple of hours later, she sat up and screamed.

14

Suki's eyes were open, but blank, like she wasn't seeing me or anything else. She kept screaming. She screamed and screamed. It scared the snow out of me. Francine ran into our bedroom wearing only a tatty T-shirt. "Oh," she said, "nightmare." She shook Suki awake and said to me, "Way Suki was hollering, I thought you two'd been attacked by wolves."

Teena's mom used to say me and Suki were being raised by wolves. She said it whenever Suki messed something up, like when Suki didn't know that when a toilet plugs, you're supposed to mash it with a plunger, and she just kept flushing until toilet water and paper and snow was pouring across the floor. The words *raised by wolves* made

Suki angry—especially when it was Teena's mom saying them, since Teena's mom was in and out of jobs and boy-friends and was generally not someone you could count on.

I liked the idea. *Raised by wolves.* Imagine how safe and warm you'd be, sleeping every night in a den full of wolves. Big teeth and all that fur. Plus, Suki pretty much *was* a wolf. She'd outfight anything. She was my own private wolf.

When Francine left, I put my arms around Suki. I said, "We're okay. We're here now." She didn't reply. "We'll get our own place," I said. "One with a great big lock on the door. Won't let nobody else have a key."

She whimpered, which frightened me more than the screams.

I said, "Suki, we're okay. It's okay here."

"I didn't know," she said.

"Doesn't matter," I said.

"I did tell someone," Suki said. "Teena asked me, 'Why didn't you tell?' I *did*. I told Stacy. She called me a liar and never wanted to be my friend again."

"Tell what?" I asked. "Who's Stacy?" I didn't know any-one named that.

Suki shook herself, and seemed to wake up a little more. "Who's Stacy?" I repeated.

"Oh." Suki blinked. "Um. Friend of mine. In fifth grade."

Didn't ring any bells. Must have been a temporary friend, like my Junebug.

"What'd you tell her?"

Suki whispered, "About Clifton."

"But fifth grade was before Mama left," I said. "Before she—you know—" *Blew up the motel room.*

"Yeah. Maybe I'm wrong. It probably wasn't fifth grade." Suki sounded wrung out. Sad and scared. "But then, that's why—I was afraid to tell anybody else. I couldn't lose Teena."

I did not understand what she was talking about. Teena was the one person who knew Clifton wasn't our dad. "We haven't lost Teena," I said. Teena'd never stop being our friend. "I been telling you. I need to see her."

Teena always jumped in to help us, and she always knew what to do. Once I spilled nail polish all over the beige rug at Clifton's house. First we tried to get it out with paper towels and then nail polish remover, but neither one worked. I was panicking 'cause it was already Thursday night and Clifton was not going to be happy when he got home Friday and saw a giant hot-pink splotch permanently in the middle of the living room. Then Teena realized the rug was a rug on both sides—the underneath looked exactly like the top. We flipped the rug over, so the stain was against the floor, and put all the furniture back. Clifton never knew.

Suki flinched. "I know. But I hate that she knows everything. Sometimes people know too much. You can't forget things when you're around them." She shut her eyes. "I just can't stand it. She looks at me different now."

I had no idea what she meant. Teena did know everything about us. Always had. That was a good thing. I lay down on my half of the pillow. "I miss her," I whispered. Suki didn't reply.

15

Next morning when I walked into our classroom, Nevaeh smiled at me.

"Alled!" she said. "Did you bring me any creamer?"

"Yoj!" I said. "I did not. I just couldn't decide between the salted caramel macchiato or the almond milk Irish crème."

She sighed. "I understand."

Then came math and it was like old times. My head felt full of sand.

At an amusement park, a group of 57 people wants to ride the roller coaster. If each car on the roller coaster holds 8 people, how many people will be in the partially full car?

Who cares?

Ms. Davonte walked past and tapped my paper. "Get to work," she said. Like my brain wasn't working if it wasn't doing math.

53, I wrote.

Ms. Davonte's lips pursed like she'd tasted something sour. "Erase that," she said. "Be better, Della."

I erased it. I wrote *2*.

Two of us on a roller coaster. Suki and me.

At recess Nevaeh and Luisa and me were standing under one of the big trees, talking, when Trevor came up and pinched Nevaeh's back. Right in the middle, a big hard pinch, a whole chunk of skin. Nevaeh flinched away from him, but she didn't even yell, much less punch him.

"Ha!" Trevor said. "Still a baby! When you going to fix that?"

Nevaeh turned away from him. She didn't say anything. She looked like she was trying not to cry.

I took a step toward Trevor. "Hey!" I said. "Knock it off!"

He whirled around. "What'd you say?"

"I said knock it off! I saw you pinch her."

"She's a baby!" he said. "I bet you're a baby too!" He stuck his tongue out at me and ran away. I looked around. None of the teachers had noticed a thing.

A gust of wind blew a handful of yellow leaves to the ground. Nevaeh's bottom lip was quivering. "Please be quiet, Della," she said.

Luisa said, "Don't make such a big deal."

"What was he even doing?" I asked. "What was that about?"

Nevaeh dropped her voice to a whisper. "He was checking to see if I'm wearing a bra."

I said, "Why the snow would you wear a bra? You're nine."

"Shh!" she said. "Stop shouting!"

"I'm not," I said, though I took it down a notch. "Why would anyone care whether you wear a bra?"

"He and his brother Daniel used to go around snapping girls' bra straps," Luisa explained. "Last year. Daniel was in sixth grade. Sixth-grade girls mostly wear bras. Trevor and Daniel thought it was funny to snap them. But then he tried with us—we don't wear bras yet. So now he pinches us and calls us babies."

"Last year you were in third grade," I said. "Doesn't sound funny to me."

Nevaeh squirmed. "Trevor thinks so. He does it to lots of girls."

"My mom says we have to ignore him," Luisa said. She pushed her glasses farther up on her nose, and shuddered. "She says he does it for attention, and if we don't give him any attention, maybe he'll stop."

"So you just let him get away with it?"

Luisa shrugged. Nevaeh said, "I tried telling our teacher last year. It made everything worse. The teacher didn't do anything, and now Trevor picks on me more."

"Are you kidding me?" I said. I looked around the playground for him. "What a snowman!"

"Jeez, Della," Nevaeh said. "You can't use words like that at school. You're gonna get us all in trouble. Calm down, okay?"

I ignored her. I marched over to where Trevor was scuffling with a bunch of boys. I grabbed him by the shoulder. "Look, snowman, you better not mess with Nevaeh again. You better not mess with anybody."

He said, "I'm telling Ms. Davonte you said *snowman*."

"Go ahead," I said. "I ain't scared of either one of you."

So he did. I spent the rest of recess inside, writing "I will not use inappropriate language at school" fifty times.

When Nevaeh came in, she frowned at me and said, "I asked you not to do that."

I said, "The way I asked you not to look at my math paper?"

Her eyes and mouth got round. "You didn't ask—"

"Because you grabbed it before I could!"

"I was helping you!" she said.

"And I helped you with Trevor!"

Nevaeh shook her head. "You didn't. You'll see. You just made things worse."

I disagreed. I'd stood up for Nevaeh the way I would have wanted someone to stand up for me.

Also, he was totally a snowman.

16

At after-school, the other girls were still cool to me. I sat with them for snacks and homework—and yeah, the math was starting to make more sense—but none of us said much, and then they all ran off to the pool and I went to the gym.

On the way home I asked Francine, "Is Suki working?"

Francine checked her watch, and nodded. "Until six."

"Can you run me by Food City? I've got something I need to buy for school."

"Sure," she said. "But Food City's not the best place for school supplies. How about Walmart?"

I shook my head. She shrugged. When we got to Food

95

City, she said, "Want me to come in with you, or want to go by yourself?"

It hadn't occurred to me that she'd come with me. "I'm fine."

"Wait." Francine dug in her purse and pulled out her wallet. "How much do you think you'll need?"

I waved my hand. "Suki'll pay for it."

"Suki hasn't gotten a paycheck yet," Francine said. "Plus, if it's something you need, it's my job to buy it. Not hers. How much?"

I shrugged. "Couple bucks."

She gave me a five. I went in and made my choice, then had Suki check me out. "What are you up to?" she asked.

"Nothing."

"Is that a present for Francine?"

"Nope."

"Huh," she said.

Next morning, when I walked into the classroom, I slapped what I'd bought down on Nevaeh's desk. I said, "Southern. Butter. Pecan."

Nevaeh eyed the jug of creamer. She eyed me. She said, deadpan, "I only like *Northern* butter pecan."

We fell over laughing, both of us. Then I said, "I'm sorry I was up in your business with Trevor."

Nevaeh said, "I'm sorry I grabbed your paper. I was only trying to help."

I nodded. "So was I."

Then Ms. Davonte told everyone to be quiet and take out a pencil. Nevaeh reached into her desk, grabbed two pencils, and handed one to me.

That felt really cool.

When I got in the car that evening, Francine handed me a backpack. "I saw it on sale when I was shopping on my lunch hour," she said. "You probably ought to have one. I got you some pencils too."

It was a pretty nice backpack. Purple, my favorite color. "It won't make Ms. Davonte like me more," I said.

I'd figured something out, which was that I looked better than I was. There were kids showed up at my new school in clothes so dirty, the teachers washed them in washing machines right there at the school. They had a closet full of clothes for kids to borrow while their stuff was being cleaned.

If I looked worse, I think Ms. Davonte might have been more patient with me. She was real nice to the kids who came into the classroom looking like snow. Me—it was like she thought a clean glitter hoodie and new high-tops meant I had no problems at all, and I should whip through my worksheets with a smile.

"Doesn't mean you don't need a backpack," Francine said. "Put that hoodie in the wash when you get home. It's getting funky."

I didn't want to wash my hoodie. It wasn't funky.

She made me do it anyway.

Suki waltzed in from her shift at Food City, all smiles. She said it had been busy and the work was easy, and one of the managers—not Tony, some other one—told her she was doing well. She said, "I love the *bing-bing-bing* noise when I'm really working fast. And I've memorized about half the numbers for the produce. But some of that stuff, I don't even know what it is. Y'all ever heard of a shallot?"

I shook my head.

"Baby onion," Suki said. "Little thing. But not like a green onion, those are different. Shallots cost about a million dollars a pound, and when I asked the woman buying them what they tasted like she said 'Onions.' I was all, then why not just get onions? They're, like, way cheaper."

She was talking super fast. I waited for her to ask about my day. To wonder what I'd done with the creamer she knew I'd bought the day before. She didn't.

"Designer food," Francine said. "Not my style." She stuck some plates on the table. She'd made meat loaf and actual mashed potatoes, from potatoes that she boiled and then mashed, and actual green beans too. It was sort of extraordinary. I was used to food that came out of a box.

I waited and waited. Suki never did ask about my day. After dinner, she went into her room, to do homework, she said. I watched TV with Francine. Suki never came out, and when I went into the bedroom, she was already asleep. She stayed asleep until two a.m., when she started to scream.

That made three nights in a row for her nightmares.

. . .

At Clifton's house Suki didn't have nightmares, even though it was scary there and never easy to sleep. When Clifton wasn't home, when it was just Suki and me, sometimes the wind would get to blowing, and the house would creak and start to shake, and even Suki would be frightened. She'd make sure all the doors were locked, one, two, three, and then she'd go around and check them again. One, two, three. Then we'd turn the TV up real loud and keep it on all night long.

Weekend nights, when Clifton was home, were even worse. Suki'd be strung so tight, her hands would shake. I'd fall asleep eventually, with Suki's arms around me, but she'd lie awake, staring into the darkness.

Sometimes when I woke up in the night, Suki wasn't in our room. Sometimes I'd think it was her screaming that woke me, or her crying, muffled, from a long way away. I'd sit up in bed and yell for her, and she'd come in, saying, "I was just using the bathroom."

Sometimes she'd be wiping tears from her face.

Sometimes she'd have a funny smell around her, one I couldn't place.

Those nights I never could go back to sleep well. I'd lie awake, and so would Suki. Those were the bad nights, the worst ones.

At school Monday mornings it would be like my whole head was full of sand. I couldn't learn anything, because nothing could get past the sand into my brain. I just sat, and words slipped by without me hearing one of them. Drove my teachers crazy.

But now—it was pretty easy to see Francine wasn't likely to hurt us, and if it came down to a fight, I figured me and Suki could take her. She was tough, but not as tough as us. So I was sleeping pretty good, except for Suki's screaming.

"What's wrong with you?" I asked her on Wednesday.

"*Nothing*," she said. "Jeez."

Thursday, the caseworker dropped off brochures: *A Guide for Teens in Foster Care* and *Independent Youth Living Handbook*. Suki didn't even glance at them. She said, "I can't have custody of Della if I'm still in foster care."

"Y'all are better off staying in care," Francine said. "Nobody's splitting you up."

Francine told the caseworker again that we needed mental health evaluations. She said, "Suki's having nightmares every night."

"I am not," Suki said, which was such a lie, Francine didn't even bother to contradict it. "I'm *fine*," Suki said. "I'm going to school and I'm working hard at my job. I work as much as they let me. I take good care of Della."

"It's not your job to take care of Della anymore," Francine said. "It's mine."

Suki gave her side-eye. I did too.

Francine said to Suki, "It's also my job to take care of you."

Suki laughed out loud.

"It is," Francine said to the caseworker, "which is why I need to insist on this. They need to be evaluated. They need counseling."

Suki put on a winsome smile. "We don't," she said. "We're doing great."

"They aren't," Francine said.

The caseworker looked from Suki to Francine and back again, like she was trying to decide who to believe. In the end she said, "Just keep me posted," and made another note in her files.

I'd prefer to believe Suki too, if she were telling the truth. I mean, I'd rather Suki was fine. But she wasn't.

"You're like a pressure cooker," Francine said, when the caseworker left, "and the water's getting hot."

Suki said, "What the snow's a pressure cooker?"

"A thing my mamaw used to have," Francine said. "For canning vegetables from her garden. It's a pot you put water in and seal tight shut before you heat it up. The water boils into steam and makes pressure.

"Thing is," Francine said, "pressure cookers have this little valve on top. Rattles around, keeps the pressure from building up too high inside the pot. If the valve isn't working right, pressure cookers can be dangerous. They can turn into bombs. They explode."

Francine looked Suki in the eye. "Trying too hard to keep everything under wraps makes you liable to explode. Getting help—therapy—that's like putting in a release valve."

Suki said, "That's the stupidest comparison I ever heard."

Francine said, "Actually, it's a pretty good one."

I thought of myself at school, trying to work with my head full of sand. I wouldn't mind a release valve. No, I would not.

17

The second Friday night I spent at Food City, I knew Nevaeh wasn't going to be there. I'd asked, and she said their SNAP benefits didn't renew for another eight days, and her mom didn't get a paycheck for six, so they wouldn't be doing any grocery shopping this week.

Nevaeh'd given me a book to read. It came out of the school library, but Nevaeh's the one who handed it to me. It was about a girl like me, in a tough spot, who was planning to steal a dog so she could give it back and get reward money. I started reading it after school while listening to Francine's neighbor's dog yap. The neighbor's dog lives on a chain behind our duplex and never stops barking. I steal the neighbor's dog, I ain't giving it back. I'm taking it far from here and leaving it.

I wouldn't be mean. I'll drop it off in a nice place, near a house that looks like it could use a small, useless, yapping dog.

I'm not one for dogs. Not one for books, either, come to that. But whatever, I took the book with me. Had to have something to do besides clean the deli.

Maybelline was working again. She slid me a cookie when I bought my Coke and said, "Where you been?"

"Nowhere," I said. "It's been boring."

She said, "You'd better be boring while you're here."

I flashed my book at her.

"Huh," said Maybelline. "That's short. It won't take you all night."

She don't know how slow I read. "Don't worry," I said. "I'll have time to help you wipe the tables."

She looked around the deli. "Be a while till we get to that. Wait until people clear out."

A customer come up and wanted half a pound of Havarti cheese, sliced thin. No, thinner than that, no, not that thin. Nobody wants cheese sliced that thin. Then a pound of sliced turkey. No, not the smoked turkey. Wasn't there turkey on sale this week? It was in the paper, cheap turkey.

After the customer left, Maybelline motioned me over. I got up, hoping for another cookie. Instead she said, "Hasn't anybody ever told you to use conditioner on your hair?"

"What's conditioner?" I asked.

She walked out from behind the deli and crossed the store to Health and Beauty next to the pharmacy. She plucked a bottle off the shelves. "Here," she said. "Slather this on your head after you shampoo. You won't have so many tangles to rip out."

That'd be a nice change. I looked at Maybelline's hair. Beautiful, all braided and done up in soft waves like wings.

I said, "I wish my hair was like yours."

She looked at me like she thought I was being sarcastic, or mean, but then she saw I meant it, and she smiled. "Thank you," she said.

I took the bottle of conditioner. It cost $3.99. I wasn't buying it with my 10 percent, but maybe I could sneak it into Francine's groceries without her noticing. "Thank *you*," I said. It felt good, to have somebody care about my hair a little bit. "It's nice of you."

Maybelline said. "Every once in a while, I'm a nice person. Wipe down the deli table, now, will you? Then after you fill the saltshakers I'll set you up some mac 'n' cheese."

I ought to tell you why Suki and me are such fans of mac 'n' cheese. Once, long time ago, I was hungry and there wasn't any food in the house at all. Suki took me over to Teena's house, next door, and Teena got out a box of macaroni and cheese and showed Suki how to cook it. You had to stir milk and margarine in with the packet of orange cheese powder, but if you didn't have milk you could use water, or extra margarine, or both. We sat on the step eating bowls

105

of macaroni 'n' cheese. Teena said, "Next time somebody goes to the grocery, make them buy a bunch of boxes of mac and cheese. Then hide some of them. That way you always have something to eat."

We did. On the night we ran away from Clifton's house, I bet we had three dozen boxes of mac 'n' cheese under our bed. And already at Francine's we've got five or six.

Boxed mac 'n' cheese is good, but the kind they serve at Food City is even better. I was just scraping the last bits of cheese sauce off my plate when I heard someone say my name, quiet. "Della." I looked up, mostly expecting Nevaeh although I wasn't really, of course.

It was Teena. At last.

18

I jumped up. I threw my arms around her and squealed. She tried to pick me up, and I tried to pick her up, and we almost knocked over a table full of pies.

"Shh," Teena said, laughing. She looked over her shoulder toward the checkout lanes. Suki couldn't see us from where she was working, I knew that.

"Why?" I said. "Why should we be quiet? I *missed* you!" I buried my head against her belly. Teena had the best soft belly.

She dragged me back to the table I was sitting at. "Suki let it slip at school that you were here with her last Friday," she said. "I thought I'd see if you were here this week too."

"How come you didn't just come to Francine's?" Teena

could drive her mom's car to get there as easily as she could to Food City.

Teena made a face. She looked good, really good—flashy earrings and green eye shadow and some pretty lip gloss. Nice painted fingernails. Teena always took care of her looks. She said, "I don't know where Francine's house is. Suki won't tell me."

"But you do see her. She keeps telling me you don't."

"Course I see her. We've got English together. Every day." Teena fiddled with one of the sugar packets from the table. "How are you, Della?"

"I really missed you," I said. "Everything's changed, like, twenty times. Twenty times in a row."

She nodded. "People taking good care of you?"

"Yeah. We're with this lady called Francine."

"I'm glad."

"You okay?" I asked.

"Yeah, sure," she said. "My mom's working. I might try to get a job, but, you know, we've only got the one car." She was smiling, but she also looked ready to cry, and I didn't know why.

"Why's Suki mad at you?" I asked. "She won't talk to me about it."

Teena hesitated. "I figured out her bad secret," she said, "the one she doesn't want anybody to know."

I didn't know what she meant by that, but before I could ask, she grabbed my hands. "Look, like I told her, you can't

be ashamed of Clifton, okay? Everything that happened—
it was on him. Okay? Not your fault and not Suki's—"

Suki said, loud and cold, "Get the snow out of this
grocery store."

I jumped. She was standing right next to us, looking
fierce.

Teena whipped around too. "Hey, Suki," she said, "I was
just checking on Della. I wanted to check on you—"

"Out," Suki said. "Get. Out."

"Suki, it's a Food City," I said. "You can't make her
leave."

"Don't worry," Teena said to me, "I'm staying."

Suki shouted, "OUT!"

"Suki!" I said.

From the corner of my eye, I could see Maybelline coming toward us, faster than I thought she could move. Even
before she reached us, another voice said, "Ladies. Is there
a problem?"

It was Tony. He didn't look like Coach Tony, or the
friendly guy who made jokes about creamer. He looked in
charge.

He looked angry.

I took a step back.

Suki said, "She needs to leave. She needs to quit talking
to my sister. I don't want her—"

Teena said, "It's a free world, Suki. This is a grocery
store!"

"GET OUT!" Suki shoved Teena's shoulders, hard. Teena stepped backwards, tripped over a chair, and sprawled across the floor.

Everyone went silent. Everyone in the entire store, or at least that's what it felt like to me.

Then Tony spoke again, his voice clipped and hard. "Suki, you're done for the night. You need to clock out and leave right now."

19

Suki ripped off her name badge and threw it onto the floor. She stalked into the office and came back a moment later, slamming the office door. She grabbed my arm. "C'mon, Della." She pulled me out of the store.

Over my shoulder, I saw Teena and Maybelline and Tony all in a little group, watching us leave, and also all the other checkout clerks and a lot of the customers, silent and staring, like they couldn't take their eyes off us. Friday night fights at Food City. Some people consider anything entertainment.

Teena put her hands up to her chest, fingers folded, making a heart shape.

"Suki," I said, "I don't want to—"

"Come *on*." Suki yanked me out by the arm.

In the car, she leaned her head against the steering wheel, breathing hard and fast. Her hands shook. I stared at her. I hadn't seen her this upset since—well, since we were getting into the back seat of the cop car. Back at Teena's house, the night we ran.

"I don't understand," I said.

She took a deep breath. "There's nothing to understand."

"But—"

She lifted her head. "Della, shut up, all right? Just shut up."

My sister never once in her life had told me to shut up.

"No!" I said. "You told me you never saw Teena anymore, and you've seen her every single day. I miss her! I was worried she didn't want to stay friends with us. I was worried she didn't care enough—"

"STOP TALKING!" Suki started the car. She stomped the gas and the whole car thumped, up, then down, front wheels, back wheels. We hit something. Or someone. I screamed.

"It's just the curb!" Suki said. The tires squealed as she yanked the car around a corner.

She was squealing tires in a Food City parking lot.

"Lemme out," I said. "You're driving crazy."

She braked hard. I tried to open the door, but she jabbed a button and the door locked. "Calm down," she said. "You're fine. Put your seat belt on."

"Why were you lying to me about Teena?"

She inched forward to a stoplight and didn't look at me. "I wasn't."

"Snow, you absolutely were." When she didn't respond, I said, "She said it's because she guessed your secret."

Her eyes flicked over to mine, then back to the road. The light changed. She swung the car onto the parkway.

She looked trapped. Panicked. *"Don't,"* she said.

"What's the secret?" I said.

"I don't have a secret," she said. "But if I did, it'd *be* a secret, right? So, none of your business."

She sped up, then had to slam on the brakes to keep from plowing into a pickup truck. "You're fine, all right? Let it go. I'm taking care of you."

"No, you aren't—"

"SHUT UP! Okay? I'm doing my best. Don't wreck things."

We pulled into Francine's driveway. Suki said, "At midnight we'll go pick up Francine. You be quiet about tonight, all right? Pretend it didn't happen. Francine doesn't need to know."

We went into Francine's house. Suki went into our bedroom and shut and locked the door. I knocked and called her name, but she ignored me.

My stomach hurt.

After a while, I turned on the TV. I lay down on the couch and fell asleep.

At midnight, Suki woke me. We got back in the car and

drove downtown. Francine was waiting outside O'Maillin's with two of her friends, all laughing like they'd had a fun night. She got into the car still laughing. I was sitting in the back seat, fiddling with my seat belt.

"You girls good?"

"We had a great night!" Suki said, in such a fake cheerful voice, I was sure Francine would know she was lying.

If she did, she didn't say anything. Neither did I. Suki drove us home, pulled into the driveway, and parked the car. We all got out. Francine walked around to the trunk.

Suki was already halfway up the front steps. Francine said, "Click the trunk, Suki. We need to grab the groceries."

Suki's face fell. "Oh. Snow. I forgot about the groceries."

"We didn't get them," I said.

Francine turned to me. "You spent the entire night at the grocery store and forgot to buy groceries?"

"Teena showed up," I said, "and Suki got mad."

"Ah." Francine studied us. Then she went inside, took off her jacket, and sprawled across the couch. "Y'all want to tell me what happened?"

Suki told the whole story, standing just inside the front door, fists clenched.

"Suki," Francine said, "calm down. We'll get groceries tomorrow. Next time something happens, just tell me straight up."

Right. Because if we caused enough trouble we'd be living somewhere else.

"Think you've still got a job?" Francine asked.

Suki shrugged. "Doubt it."

"What on earth were you thinking?"

"I told Teena to mind her own business," Suki said. "I told her to stay away from Della, and me—"

"Suki," I said, "*what happened?*"

She whirled on me. "What do you mean, 'what happened?' You know what happened! Our mother went away and left us with a monster! We had to live with him! For five years! That's what happened. You know it, Della. You were there."

I wouldn't have used the word *monster*. Not until the night we ran.

Suki went out the front door. Francine went after her. Suki was sitting on the front step, her head in her hands. She was crying.

Francine said, "I think I better talk to your caseworker. I'll call her Monday. When are you scheduled to work again?"

Suki grimaced. "Monday."

"Okay." Francine touched Suki's shoulder. Suki flinched. "Come inside and go to bed. This'll pass."

While I was in the bathroom brushing my teeth, I pulled a deli napkin out of my hoodie pocket. As soon as Suki'd gone into the office, Teena'd whipped a pen out of her purse, scrawled something on a napkin, and thrust the napkin at me. I'd stuffed it in my pocket, quick, before Suki came out.

Now I unfolded and looked at it. A phone number. Teena's phone number.

I sat down on the toilet seat and read the number over until I knew it by heart. Then I wadded the napkin up and stuck it in the back corner of the cabinet under the sink, behind a stack of toilet paper, just in case.

I went into the bedroom. Suki was in the upper bunk, on top of the blankets, still fully dressed. She was staring at the ceiling. "Do you mind sleeping in the bottom bunk tonight?"

I minded. Of course I minded. "Why?"

"I just want to be by myself. I want to be alone."

I didn't. But I crawled into the lower bunk anyway. I could hear my own heart beating. Francine's house didn't seem safe anymore. Neither did my sister.

20

In the morning when I got up, Francine was already in the kitchen, drinking coffee. "Hey, kiddo," she said.

"Hey." I poured myself some raisin bran and sat down to eat it.

"You want milk with that?"

"No." I like my cereal crunchy.

She sat down at the table next to me. "Don't panic," she said. "We're all okay."

"How much trouble is too much trouble?" I asked. "For you to keep us."

Francine shook her head. "Way more than this." She said, "Nobody gets put in foster care for happy reasons. It's always hard. I understand why you and Suki might be angry."

"I'm not angry," I said.

"Whatever you feel."

"I'm fine."

When Suki got up, we all went back to Food City. Francine drove. When we got there, Francine and I started shopping and Suki went into the office. When she came back to us, her face was blank.

"Well?" said Francine.

"Nothing," Suki said.

"No job?"

"No consequences," she said. "None of the day managers even knew anything had happened. Tony didn't write me up." She shook her head. "I'm still working after school next week. But he took me off the schedule for next Friday."

Francine said, "He's giving you another chance."

"Why would he?"

I said, "Maybe because he's the nicest man in the world."

Maybelline wasn't working the deli counter, but when we walked through Health and Beauty, I remembered the conditioner she told me to buy. I pulled it off the shelf and showed it to Francine.

"That's fine," Francine said. "Whatever it is you think you need."

"Even though it costs three ninety-nine?" We weren't getting any 10 percent treats this week. Suki only got a discount during her shifts.

Francine sighed like she'd had about all she could take

of Suki and me. "I told you I was doing this for the money," she said.

"So you don't want to spend any on us."

"No. That is not what I mean." Francine drew herself up a little. "I'm getting paid to do a job," she said. "That job is to take care of you. That means getting you whatever you need. Clothes, haircuts, doctor, dentist. Lawyers, case-workers. Therapists. Everything. If your hair needs special stuff, then it's part of my job to see you get it."

Suki grumbled, "Della don't need special stuff."

"My hair's different from yours!"

Suki looked angry. "I always took care of you just fine."

I took a deep breath and blew it out. "Just because you always did your best doesn't mean I can't use conditioner."

Suki glared at me. I glared back. "It's just *conditioner*," I said. I ought to be allowed to say that.

At school Monday morning I made Nevaeh mad again. It started when I gave her back the book.

"Did you read it?"

I nodded. It was how I'd spent most of Sunday after-noon. Suki and Francine had hardly paid me any attention at all.

"How'd you like it?" Nevaeh asked.

"Eh. It was okay."

Her eyebrows shot up. "Just okay? It's better than *okay*." She sounded annoyed. "I loved it."

"It wasn't really a happy ending," I said. "I mean, they didn't have to live in their car anymore, and the dog was back home, but everything was still all unsettled. They might have had to go back to that car anytime. Those friends might not want to keep helping them. It wasn't really better. Not *permanent*."

Nevaeh looked downright angry. "It was a *lot* better than living in their *car*," she said. "They got to sleep on, like, actual beds."

"Well, sure," I said. "But—"

"You've never had to live in a car, have you?"

"Well, no," I said, "but—"

Ms. Davonte clapped her hands for attention then, with a special glare at me when I tried to keep talking to Nevaeh. I knew I'd gone wrong with Nevaeh and I had no idea where. Sometimes it seemed like everybody understood the rules but me.

At recess, I followed Nevaeh out to the playground. She sat down on a swing and I sat next to her. "You were right," I said. "I've been thinking about it. It was a really good book."

She looked at me. "You're just saying that."

"No, I mean it!"

"What changed your mind?"

I took a deep breath, and went with the truth. "I want us to be friends. If that means I have to like the book, then I really, really like the book."

She stared at me for a moment, then laughed. She said, "You don't have to like everything I like. It's just—that book is really important to me." After a pause she said, "We lost our apartment a few years ago, after my dad left. Mom and me. We're doing a lot better now."

I could hear what she was saying even without her saying it. I said it for her. "You had to live in a car."

"Only for a couple of nights. But I hated it." She drew a circle in the dirt with her toe. "I was glad, you know, to read the book. To know it didn't only happen to me."

I used my toe to draw a circle beside hers. "My sister was always afraid we'd be out on the streets. Only we didn't have a car."

There were, like, a hundred kids on the playground. Running all around us, yelling and laughing, kicking balls. But it felt like it was just Nevaeh and me.

"Were you afraid?" she asked.

I shook my head. "No. I knew Suki would take care of me." She always did.

"My mom takes care of me," Nevaeh said. "My mom takes *really good* care of me. But we still lost that apartment."

"Where do you live now?"

"A different apartment. I told you, we're better now."

"We're better now too," I said. "Suki and me." I took another deep breath. "We're in foster care. Francine, she's what they call a foster mother."

Nevaeh's eyes widened. "Foster care is better than what you had before?"

"Yep," I said.

"Wow," she said. "That's hard." She sounded like Francine.

"Yep," I said. "It is."

That night, Suki came home from work and went straight to bed. When I went to call her to dinner, she had the covers over her head and was sound asleep.

"Leave her," Francine said. "She won't starve overnight."

Later I crawled in to sleep beside her. When I woke up to go pee, she was wide awake, staring at the ceiling.

"You okay?" I asked.

"Sure," she said.

A couple hours later she started screaming. We were used to it by now.

21

The next afternoon, when we were supposed to be working on math problems, Trevor got up and started walking toward the back of the class. Going to sharpen his pencil, I supposed. As he passed Nevaeh's desk, he reached out and pinched the middle of her back. Again. Nevaeh jumped, but didn't make a sound.

I stuck my foot sideways, fast. I caught Trevor right between the legs and he tripped, sprawling onto the floor. He got up, ready to take a swing at me. "She kicked me!" he shouted.

"Sorry, Trevor," I said. "It was an accident. Don't be such a *baby*."

Trevor's face turned red. I looked at Nevaeh. Her face

had gone bright red too. She hunched her shoulders and stared at her desk.

Ms. Davonte came over. "Della," she said.

"I didn't kick him," I said. "I maybe tripped him but it was only by accident. I promise."

"Keep your feet to yourself, Della," Ms. Davonte said.

"Snow!" I said. "What about Trevor's hands? He pinched Nevaeh!"

Whoops. I hadn't meant to say that. Nevaeh lifted her chin and glared at me.

"Sorry," I mouthed.

It didn't matter. Ms. Davonte only paid attention to one word I said, and you can guess which word it was. I had to stay in at recess, and Ms. Davonte gave me another note for Francine to sign. "Della," Ms. Davonte said, "when are you going to learn to watch your mouth?"

She never realizes. I watch my mouth all the time.

When I got on the bus for after-school, Nevaeh had an empty seat beside her. I stood in the aisle, not sure she'd want me near her.

"Oh, sit down," she said.

"I didn't mean it," I said.

"You did. You tripped him. I saw you."

"Well, yeah, I meant *that*," I said. "I didn't mean to say he'd pinched you, though. I know you don't want me to."

She nodded. "I don't. Also you cuss worse than every-body else in our class combined."

Trevor got onto the bus and threw himself down in the front seat, where the bus driver made him sit. He was laughing. "They're words," I said to Nevaeh. "Everybody gets upset, but cuss words are just *words*. He's hurting you. He shouldn't be allowed to do that."

"I don't want you fighting my fights for me, Della. It's my business. Not yours."

"But you don't fight," I said.

She sighed. "It's not that big of a deal."

It was to me.

22

Suki fought for me, and I'm fighting for me, and that's why Clifton is in jail. There's going to be a trial, and it's going to be easy because we have evidence, and hard because it's scary and because having to testify against Clifton sucks. But the truth is, I got off easy. What he did was the worst few minutes of my life up until that time. But it only lasted a few minutes. Hard, easy, hard, easy.

Hard hard hard.

What Clifton did to me is still not the hardest part of this story.

Anyhow, I'm getting ahead of myself. The next Wednesday, I had to go to—I don't know what you call it, the official name. It's a place kids go to tell stories like mine, when there's going to be a trial. Because I was young enough and this stuff is hard enough that I could tell the story somewhere other than court. They would film me talking and show the video in court, instead of me having to testify in person.

The place was an old house, set back in woods, with a swing set on the lawn. Suki and our other caseworker, whose name I never remember any better than the first one, but who's setting up the trial stuff, took me there on Wednesday after school.

Right from the start, Suki was tense and watchful and fierce. She held my hand when we walked into the building, and she sat right beside me in the waiting room, so close, our legs touched. She said, "Are you going to be okay?"

My mouth was dry. I nodded.

They took me upstairs alone. I sat on an upholstered chair. My legs didn't quite touch the floor. The woman there explained the video camera and how everything about the trial would work, and yeah, yeah, I already understood all that.

My heart was beating faster than usual. I don't know why. Nothing could hurt me, not in that room with Suki right downstairs.

I told my story. I explained the photograph the woman handed me, the one printed out from Teena's phone. I explained how the photograph got to Teena's phone. I explained about Clifton, how we lived with him, how I knew we were supposed to keep it secret that we really didn't belong to him.

"Why did you keep it secret?" the woman asked. I could tell she was asking so my answer would be recorded. She didn't really want to know.

"Suki said we had to," I said. "Also, we didn't have anywhere else to go. We had to live somewhere."

By this time, my hands were shaking and I felt a little sick. Remembering what happened, thinking about it, that's hard, but not nearly as hard as seeing the picture and talking about it.

"Good job," the woman said, turning off the camera. "You did great, Della. You were very brave."

Then we went back downstairs. Suki jumped up and hugged me tight. The woman said to Suki, "Your turn."

Suki went white, like all the blood in her body suddenly drained below her knees. She went stiff too, and her voice sounded angry. "What for? I took the photo, didn't I? You know that."

"Yes," the woman said, very softly. "I need you to talk about taking the photograph. On camera, for the court."

"Just that, right?" Suki said. "'Cause I ain't—I ain't—"

I should have seen it right then, the whole truth, in the rigid set of Suki's jaw. In the way her voice shook. If her nightmares and the stuff with Teena hadn't been enough already.

I should have realized.

"Just that," the woman said. "Unless—"

Suki shook her head hard, once, no. She clamped onto my hand. "I want Della with me."

So upstairs again, and this time I sat on a plain chair in the corner while Suki sat in the pink upholstered chair. She sounded angry and snotty, and she said *snow, snowing, snowflake, snowmen* a whole lot. The woman running the camera kept trying to be nice, and Suki kept batting her kindness aside. Her voice was bitter and tight.

Afterward the woman thanked her. She said, "I can't imagine how hard it was for you. You being so little, trying to take care of your sister, all alone so much of the time. You were too young for that kind of responsibility."

I'd never thought about it as worse for Suki than me. Suki was so strong. I said, "It was a lot better when Clifton was gone than when he was at home."

The woman gaped at me. Suki said, "You're snow right," and grabbed my hand and hauled me down the stairs.

That was the end of what we were going to have to do for the trial.

Or so I thought.

23

That night, at dinner, I asked Francine, "How much time is Clifton gonna get?"

Francine said, "All goes well—and it should—a couple of years."

"Really?" I said. I knew what he did was bad. Just thinking about it made me feel sick. But I didn't know if people actually went to prison for that kind of thing.

Suki dropped her fork. She said, "That's ALL?"

"According to the guidelines," Francine said. "That's what your lawyer thinks, anyhow. What were you expecting?"

I didn't expect much. Also, I never listened to the lawyers. I tried, but mostly when people were talking about Clifton, it was like my head filled up with bees all buzzing at once. I couldn't make out a single word.

Suki said a lot of words about snow.

Francine said, "It was only the one time, right? And only what you caught in the photo?"

Suki glared at me. I said, "Yep." Which was the truth. Thank God.

Then Francine said, "I meant for both of you," and Suki's face crumpled. I remembered that, later.

We've come to the part of the story where I've got to tell you what happened. What happened to me.

It was a Thursday night. That mattered. Clifton drove away in his truck on Monday mornings, before I even left for school, and he never, but never, got back before Friday afternoon. Sometimes it was even later—sometimes, if the weather was bad or there were accidents on the highway or something, it might even be Saturday, but it was never Thursday. Thursday nights were good nights.

Teena and some of Suki's other friends wanted Suki to go to a movie with them. You can't walk to the movie theater from where we lived—you really couldn't walk to anywhere—but Teena had borrowed her mom's car and there was some movie they all wanted to see, some superhero thing.

Suki said, "We gotta take Della."

Teena said, "We don't have room in the car, Suki. Not with all of us going. What's she going to do, ride in the trunk?"

I'd done that once, but I'd been smaller then. It hadn't been as much fun as I thought it would be.

"Plus," said Teena, "the movie's rated R. No way they're going to let Della in."

"Plus I don't want to go," I said. I thought it sounded stupid.

"It's *Thursday*," Teena said.

"Right," said Suki. Even then she was undecided. She dug around in her purse and in my backpack and in the couch cushions for the change that fell out of Clifton's pockets sometimes, and then she went over to the washing machine and looked through the stuff she'd pulled from Clifton's pockets before she did the laundry that week, and there was a twenty-dollar bill, so she had money enough for the show.

"Go," I said. "I don't mind." I didn't. It was late August, a clear night, and nice and warm. I could sit on the back step till the mosquitoes came out at dusk, and I had something to snack on and I just really didn't mind. Suki usually left me by myself when she had something she had to do. Sometimes I liked being alone.

Teena said, "My mom'll be around if she needs anything."

Suki gave me a kiss. She promised, "I'll be home by nine."

Clifton came home at 8:30.

I was wearing my purple shortie pajamas.

It was a Thursday. I never did find out why he came home on a Thursday.

Clifton banged the front door. He looked at me in a way that made me jump to my feet, though I couldn't have said why. "I'm just going to bed," I said.

"Where's your sister?"

"Sleeping."

He'd never touched me once before. I'd still never trusted him. Right then, in that instant, I knew not to trust him at all. The hairs rose up on my neck and stayed that way, like spines.

He said, "She's not here, is she?"

He smiled the way he did when he was just about to say something mean.

I looked at the clock. It was only 8:30. Thirty minutes until Suki came home. I listened for Teena's mom's car, but couldn't hear anything. My stomach hurt.

"You owe me," Clifton said. "That's what I tell your sister. You owe me, living here."

I didn't know then about people like Francine, people who would never love you but at least would keep you safe. Safe-ish.

Clifton gave us food and shelter, but we were never once safe with him.

"I'm just going to bed," I said again.

He walked forward. I backed up. He came forward. I backed up. My legs hit the living room wall.

I was trapped.

Clifton put his hand on my leg, on the inside of my thigh. Grabbed the bare skin beneath the bottom of my pajama shorts.

"Don't!" I yanked myself sideways.

He laughed. Put one thick hand around my neck. Grabbed the elastic band of my pajama shorts with the other. Stuck his hand down the back of the shorts.

Inside my underwear.

I screamed. Not that anyone was going to hear me.

"Hold still," he said.

I tried to get away.

He took hold of the waistband of my shorts, and pulled them down.

My underwear too.

Now I was crying. "Please don't—" I didn't know what he'd do next, not really, but I knew for sure I didn't want it to happen. "Please!"

Click.

I looked up, and there was Suki, standing in the doorway, holding her phone in front of her.

Taking photographs.

Click click click click.

I still couldn't move. Clifton looked sideways. He let out a roar and ran at Suki.

She jumped back outside. I dove at Clifton's legs, tripped him up. Only for a second, but that was long enough.

He yanked the door open, grabbed Suki's phone,

smashed it onto the concrete step, stepped on it with his heavy boots. I heard it break into pieces.

Suki said, "Della, run. Teena's house."

I pulled my pants back up. Ran out the back door and sprinted across the yard. Suki caught up with me. She grabbed my hand. We ran, ran, ran to Teena's house, up the steps to her front porch.

Teena threw open the screen door. She said, "Girlfriend, what the snow? What the snow did you just text me?"

"Resend it," Suki said. "Don't delete it. Resend it fast before he comes and breaks your phone too. He tried to hurt Della. I'm not going to let him."

Teena's mom came out to the porch. She looked at the photograph. "Get in the house," she said. We did. Teena's mom locked the door. She said, "Teena, go lock the back door." She picked up her own phone. She dialed 911.

"Please," Suki said, grabbing her arm, "don't call the cops."

Teena's mom shook her off.

"Please," Suki said. She started to cry. She looked frantic. "Please, don't—"

Teena said, "Mom, they can just live here!"

Teena's mom called them anyhow. Police showed up, saw the photograph, started asking questions. Suki cried and cried and then threw up and then called Teena's mother a whole bunch of hateful names. Eventually it ended just like the night of the motel fire. Clifton went away in one police car, handcuffed. Suki and I went away in another, holding hands. "It'll be okay," I whispered, over and over, but I could see Suki didn't believe me.

That's when we got that emergency foster placement witch, and after that Francine.

I still haven't told you the worst part of the story.

It's coming. Just not yet.

24

Thursday morning, the Southern butter pecan creamer was on my desk. Still unopened. Nevaeh was sitting at her desk with her face a little turned away from me.

I said, "You don't want it?"

She turned back to me, and I saw that she was smiling. "I'm giving you custody," she said. "For now."

I grinned in relief. "I can't believe you haven't finished it."

She said, "How do you know that's the same bottle?" Then she added, "My mom doesn't drink coffee. I don't think you can pour that stuff into a Coke."

I tucked the creamer into my desk. "We could try."

"You try," Nevaeh said. "Want to spend the night at my house tomorrow? My mom said you could."

"Oh." Wow. I knew people did things like that. Friends did things like that. I just never had. I said, "I think I have to ask Francine."

"Well, sure," Nevaeh said. "That's how it works. Give me her phone number, and tonight my mom will call and ask her."

"Okay." This was all new. I said, "Sometimes I don't know the rules."

"I usually do," Nevaeh said. "You can always ask me."

Suki said, "No."

"Suki!"

"We don't know anything about these people," Suki said. "We don't know who all lives in their house. We don't know what sort of stuff they get up to."

"It's just Nevaeh and her mom," I said.

"You don't know that for sure," Suki said.

"I'll ask," Francine said. "That's my job." She looked at Suki. "It's also my decision to make. Not yours." Back to me. "Della, do you want to go?"

"*Yes*," I said. "What, Suki, you're working again anyway. It's not like we'd do anything fun." I liked Food City, and Maybelline, but not as much as being with Nevaeh.

"I'd know where you were," she said. "I'd know you were safe."

"You'll know where I am," I said. "I'll be with Nevaeh.

And her mom. That's plenty safe." When she didn't answer, I said, "A real mom, Suki."

Suki just glared at me.

When Nevaeh's mom called, Francine asked her all sorts of personal questions and also made sure she knew I was a foster kid. She said saying that was part of the rules for foster care. She also said Suki'd be working at Food City and she herself would be out with friends, but she gave Nevaeh's mom her phone number and said she'd come get me anytime for any reason.

I could not imagine a reason that would make me call Francine.

"You could do it too," I said to Suki. "You could go stay at Teena's house when your shift was over."

"Not Teena—"

"One of your other friends." When she glared at me, I said, "We get to do stuff like this now, Suki."

She said, "I didn't know you were desperate to be away from me."

I said, "Says the person who put me in after-school without asking."

So. Francine told us to knock it off. Suki and I didn't speak to each other the rest of the night. Until two a.m., when she woke up screaming again and I sang "Skinna-marinky" until she fell back asleep.

■ ■ ■

Friday morning, I filled my backpack with pajamas and clean underwear and my toothbrush and stuff. When I got to school Nevaeh said, "Did you finally remember your swimsuit?"

She'd reminded me, like, sixty times. I put my backpack in my cubby in our classroom. "I don't have a swimsuit," I said. "I've never had one. I've never once been in a swimming pool."

Nevaeh laughed. "Why didn't you say so? They've got a bunch of old suits in the pool office. They won't mind if you take one."

I nearly made a face—aren't used swimsuits even skankier than used shoes?—but lucky I didn't, because she added, "That's where I got mine."

Swimming—scary, possibly creepy. I looked at Nevaeh, grinning. I said, "Okay."

Turns out used swimsuits aren't as skanky as used shoes. Pool water has chlorine in it, which is the same stuff that's in bleach, so the used suits were faded and ugly, but they smelled really clean. The person in the swimming pool office helped me dig through the box and find a suit that would probably fit. Nevaeh and Luisa and I changed in the locker room. I got into the swimsuit as fast as I could, and even then it felt strange not to be wearing more clothes.

"Is it going to be like a bathtub?" I asked. Clifton's house didn't have a bathtub, and neither did Francine's, but anytime you saw a bathtub on TV, it was full of bubbles and the people in it looked warm and comfy.

Nevaeh raised her eyebrows at me. "Sure," she said.

Luisa was stuffing her hair into a plastic cap. She said, "I mean, not really—"

Nevaeh said, "The best thing to do is just jump right in!" She grabbed my hands and jumped and pulled me in with her.

Into the coldest water in the universe.

I swear, there were icebergs floating in that pool.

I stood up, sputtering, my toes barely touching the bottom and my ears about to freeze and fall off. Nevaeh laughed and laughed. "Your face," she said. "Your face."

Meanwhile Luisa was climbing down the ladder, inch by inch, grimacing.

"Don't they heat swimming pools?" I asked. I liked my showers hot.

Luisa said, "They say they do. It never feels like it."

Nevaeh said, "You get used to it. And it really is better to jump in all at once."

"Sort of." Luisa pinched her nose shut and launched herself off the middle of the ladder. She went all the way under and came up laughing.

There was an inflatable slide at one end of the pool. We climbed up it and slid down and landed in water deeper than my head. I couldn't touch the bottom and I couldn't get my mouth out of the water and I was going to drown right there. Nevaeh grabbed my arm and pulled me to where it was shallower. On the side of the pool one of the counselors blew a whistle at me. "No more slide until you know how to swim."

Okay. Drowning, not fun. Luisa got some float boards for us and showed me how to hold on to one and kick. Kick, kick, across the pool. It was sort of like dribbling a basketball. Then we practiced in the shallow end without the boards, sort of hopping and flailing and splashing around. I wasn't swimming, but I could sort of understand how swimming might feel. I could maybe do it, if I kept practicing.

Nevaeh's mom picked the two of us up from the Y. She looked worn out, but she smiled when she saw us, and she kissed Nevaeh. That was, like, real mom behavior. What you saw on TV.

"Sorry to say this," she said as she swung out of the parking lot, "but we're going to have to stop at Food City. I haven't got a thing at home to feed you girls."

I started laughing. It was so perfect. Friday night. With a friend. At Food City.

"Mom," Nevaeh said, "Food City is where the creamer is. It's Della's favorite place in the world."

First thing we did, while Nevaeh's mom was getting a cart, was say hi to Suki. She smiled at us, but she didn't hug me and she didn't quit scanning groceries. "I'm on the clock," she said.

I pointed to Nevaeh's mom. "Look," I said, "she's totally normal."

Suki rolled her eyes.

Next we ran to the deli to see Maybelline. She grinned too. "How are you?" she asked as she got us cookies.

"Great." My hair was still wet from swimming, but I held a piece out to her. "You probably can't tell, but I am using conditioner. So, thanks. I can't stay to help you tonight," I added. "Sorry."

Maybelline said, "It's okay. I'm glad you stopped by."

After that, Nevaeh and I spent a little time playing hop-scotch on the floor tiles in the produce section. We fell into a stand of navel oranges and knocked a bunch down and had to chase after them as they rolled away.

Tony walked over while we were still stacking the oranges back into a pyramid. "Hey, sunshines," he said, smiling. "Good to see you two. Did you enjoy your free cookies?"

I nodded. Nevaeh reached into the vegetable display. She pulled out a big brown lump of a vegetable and asked Tony what it was.

"That," Tony said, "is a rutabaga."

"What do you do with it?"

"Honestly?" Tony said. "I have no idea."

This made us laugh. So did the strawberry cheesecake creamer in the next aisle. We were still giggling when we caught up to Nevaeh's mom. She smiled at us and said, "Get it together, girls."

Nevaeh was carrying the rutabaga. She stuck it in the cart when her mom wasn't looking. Her mom didn't notice it, not even when we got to the checkout. It was Suki who grabbed it and rolled her eyes at me and made me run put it back where it belonged.

When we got to the apartments where Nevaeh and her mom lived, Nevaeh and I helped carry the groceries up the stairs. Nevaeh showed me where to hang my wet swimsuit in the bathroom since they didn't have a dryer.

In the kitchen, Nevaeh's mom was making sandwiches. I opened the refrigerator and looked inside.

"Della," Nevaeh's mom said, "that's kind of rude."

"Oh." I shut the door. I looked at the ground. I didn't know.

Nevaeh said, "Sometimes you've got to tell Della the rules."

Nevaeh's mom said, "Well, I just did," in a perfectly normal voice, which made me feel better. "Are you that hungry?" she asked. "I'll have something ready for us soon."

"Not really," I said. "I just wondered what, you know, normal families ate."

Nevaeh's mom laughed. "Oh, honey. There's no such thing as a normal family."

We stayed up past midnight, all three of us, watching weird stuff on TV. Nevaeh's mom made a big bowl of popcorn that we shared. Afterward, Nevaeh and I rolled up in blankets on the living room floor and turned out the lights and talked until she fell asleep mid-sentence, her mouth closing on her final word. I wadded my pillow under my head, stretched my legs long, and went to sleep too. It was the first night I'd ever spent away from Suki. I felt fine.

No one screamed in the night. In the morning, Nevaeh's mom made us pancakes. It was, like, the best time ever.

25

When I got home, Suki was in a terrible mood. She'd gotten her schedule for the week, and she was only working six hours. Monday and Thursday. "I told them I wanted every Friday!" she said. "I'm not going to screw up again."

She'd spent her 10 percent from buying Francine's groceries on jet-black hair dye, of all things. She looked like a vampire. I didn't say so. I tried telling her about Nevaeh's house.

"Look," she said, "I'm really not interested. Okay? I saw you with them. I know you were having a great time. Good for you."

She didn't sound glad. She said, "Teena came in again. Looking for you."

Uh-oh. "Did you have another fight?"

"I didn't say a single word to her. I'm not getting fired over Teena. But she'd better leave you alone."

I thought of Teena's phone number, safe inside my memory as well as on the napkin beneath the bathroom sink. I watched Suki prowl through the house, scowling.

I couldn't call Teena on the landline, not without Suki hearing. I went to Francine. "Can I borrow your cell phone? I want to text my friend." I didn't say which friend.

I texted Teena. I'M OKAY. THANKS. HOW ARE YOU?

A minute later I got a reply. WHO IS THIS?

DELLA. FRANCINE'S PHONE.

She sent back a heart emoji and NOW IT'S IN MY CONTACTS. I CAN CHECK ON YOU.

I gave the phone back to Francine. She opened up the messages and read what I'd sent.

"Hey!" I said.

"My phone," she said. She put it back in her pocket.

"What?" asked Suki.

"Nothing," I said.

A whole week went by in which I didn't use snow words or get in a fight with Trevor. I did my homework at the Y, and then I went swimming with Nevaeh and Luisa, every day, even though I sometimes missed Coach Tony and basketball.

Suki went to school, worked her two shifts, and slept. That's all. I don't know if she did homework. I don't know if she even had homework. She used to, sometimes.

Her face was getting thinner, sharper. She woke up screaming every night. Francine called our social worker about her, but went into her bedroom to make the call. I stood right outside the closed door but couldn't hear a thing she said.

We were worried about Suki. Just not worried enough.

On Friday when Francine and I got home, Suki was already sound asleep in bed. Francine frowned. "You going to be okay with your sister tonight?"

"We're fine," I said. "I don't mind you going out. I can get us some dinner."

Francine nodded. "There's leftovers in the fridge. Call me if you need anything."

While Francine got ready to go out, I went to check on Suki. She was wrapped in a blanket on the top bunk. I poked her.

"Go away!" she said.

After Francine left, I watched TV for a little bit and then I went and poked Suki again. "Hey!" I said. "Want to make us some mac 'n' cheese?"

Suki woke up and sat up and roared. "Do I have to do EVERYTHING for you?" she shouted. "Can't you even make yourself mac 'n' cheese?"

I took a step back. My stomach dropped. Tears pricked the corners of my eyes. "No, Suki—"

"You're ten years old! I had to take care of you my whole snow life! I had to take care of you when I was *six*! It was too much, all right? I was too little! *When is somebody going to take care of me?"*

I was crying hard by then, tears just pouring down my face. "Suki," I gasped.

"Just leave me alone," she said. "Just for today, okay? Just go away and leave me alone." She threw the blanket over her head.

I went away. I left her alone.

I wish I hadn't.

I made a box of mac 'n' cheese. It turned out lousy. The noodles were still crunchy, and I didn't drain them enough, so the cheese sauce was too thin. I ate the whole box anyway. It didn't ease the ache in my stomach. Friday nights were our worst nights, always. I wished Suki and me were at Food City.

If I'd known how, I would have made popcorn. A big bowl. Maybe if I did, Suki would wake up and we'd watch a stupid movie, our hands colliding with each other's in the popcorn bowl.

Francine's house was nothing like Clifton's, but I felt like I was back in Clifton's house.

Somewhere around nine o'clock, I heard Suki crying. I went into the bedroom and climbed into the bunk beside her.

"I hate Fridays," she said.

"I know." I tried to cuddle her. She pushed me away. "Please don't touch me tonight," she said. "Please just leave me alone."

I held out my hand, fingers splayed. She kept her hands beneath the covers. "C'mon," I said. "Skinny-ma-rinky—"

"Not. Tonight." Suki rolled over, her face toward the wall.

I went back into the living room. I dug in my backpack and found a book I'd forgotten about, from the school library. All about wolves. I read it. Wolves lived in big families called packs. They used to be endangered but they were doing better now.

Eventually I climbed into the bottom bunk. Suki was snoring above me. I fell asleep before Francine came home. I thought things were mostly all right.

I couldn't have been more wrong.

26

I woke up in the middle of the night because I needed to pee. I checked the upper bunk. Suki wasn't there. I put my hand under the covers. The bed wasn't warm.

Where was she? I felt the hairs on my arms stand on end.

The alarm clock on the dresser read 2:48. We were past Suki's usual screaming time. I walked into the hallway, quiet as I could. Francine always left the light over the stove on all night. I could see Suki sitting on a chair next to the kitchen table.

On the table was a knife.

It was one of Francine's kitchen knives, long and sharp. One she cuts onions with. She had used it to make dinner on Thursday and then I helped dry the dishes and I put the

151

knife back in the drawer, but now it was in the center of the table. Suki was huddled up on the chair, arms around the top of her knees, staring at the knife like it was the best thing in the world, or the worst. Like she didn't dare look away. Like the knife was some sort of evil thing, with a spell on it maybe; like it was singing a song only Suki could hear.

The spit dried up in my mouth. I didn't move. I remembered a scene I once saw in a movie, when someone ended up right in front of a poisonous snake. Move, and the snake would strike. Don't move, same thing.

I don't think Suki heard me. She didn't look up. I stood as still as I could, barely breathing. In one part of my brain everything was whirling around. I didn't know what to do. But in another part, things were clicking into place. All the little signs I'd noticed but not understood. All the pain in Suki's face. All the nights she couldn't sleep. All the days she slept too much.

The price of our staying with Clifton was Suki.

What he'd done to me was just a tiny piece of what he'd done to her.

Even with what happened right after, that moment, that knowing, was the very worst thing. This is it. The most awful part of my story:

Clifton hurt Suki for years.

Suki looked up and saw me. She grabbed the knife, quick and hard. I yelled, "SUKI!"

She plunged the knife down.

Snow, snow, snow. If it had ended worse, then that knife, Suki wielding it, would have been the worst thing, of course, but even so, that moment right there was the second-worst thing. It was and is and always will be amazingly snowing hard.

27

Blood splurted like it was coming out a nozzle. Suki stared at it, dazed. I lunged toward her. The knife clattered to the floor. I hollered, "FRANCINE!"

She ran in. "Oh, SNOWFLAKES!" she yelled. She grabbed a kitchen towel, smacked it against Suki's wrist, and held on tight. "Della," she said, "Call 911." So it was me that made the phone call.

The ambulance people wrapped tighter bandages around Francine's towel. They strapped Suki into a stretcher and heaved her into an ambulance. Then they told Francine there was only room for one of us to ride along.

"Don't be ridiculous," Francine said. "We're both going. Della, climb in."

Suki hadn't said a single word. She still didn't. On one side of her stretcher the EMT did stuff to her wrist, trying to get it to stop bleeding. I knelt on the other side, my head against her chest.

"I'm sorry, I'm sorry, I'm sorry," I sobbed.

Suki didn't move. But she was still breathing. She didn't die.

She didn't die in the ambulance and she didn't die in the hospital.

Suki didn't die even though she'd slashed an artery. Francine said she'd had amazingly bad luck, slicing it open so wide, but I thought she just had really good aim. They had to take her into surgery to fix it, cut her arm open a little more so they could put stitches in or something, who knows, I'd quit listening by then. I stopped listening right around the time the doctor said "She's going to be okay." My ears quit working and my hands went numb and I swear I might have fallen down except that the doctor put her arms around me, right there in the waiting room, and held me up. She talked and talked. It was a good thing Francine was there to listen, 'cause I couldn't.

Hours later they let us see her. She was in bed in a room by herself, her head propped up on pillows, asleep. Her left arm was all wrapped in bandages. Her right arm had an IV line with medicine dripping into it.

"She's pretty sedated," the nurse said. "Don't expect much."

I sat down on the edge of the bed and stared at her until she opened her eyes.

"I'm sorry," she whispered.

"I'm sorry too," I said. "I'm so sorry." I leaned against her. "Please don't leave."

"I don't want to," she said. "I really don't." A pause while her eyelids fluttered shut. She opened them again, and reached for my hand. "I just wanted things to stop hurting. Just for one minute. I just couldn't—but as soon as I did it I wished I hadn't. I wanted to take it back."

"If I hadn't woke up—"

"I would have yelled," she said. "I think I would have called for help. I hope so."

"Does it hurt?"

"My wrist hurts." Suki closed her eyes. "My brain hurts. Everything. Hurts so much." By the end her words were slurring.

"Don't leave me," I said again, though I don't think she could hear.

A different doctor came in and started talking to Francine about how, now that they'd fixed Suki's arm, they needed to treat the stuff going wrong in her brain that made her want to hurt herself like that.

I knew what had gone wrong. "Clifton," I said. Also Mama. Also me.

My fault, said a voice inside my head. A horrible voice. Persistent. *My fault. Myfaultmyfaultmyfault.*

If I'd been nicer, or hadn't gone to Nevaeh's. If I'd realized what Clifton was doing. Or if I'd let him do it to—

No. Not that.

If I could have kept Suki safe. The way she kept me.

"I've been trying and trying to get her help," Francine said. "I've begged the state for mental health care. *Snow*."

The doctor looked sympathetic. "We'll take care of her now."

"And her sister," Francine said. "They'd better agree to some therapy. Kids don't come through what they did without damage. Jeez, you'd think we'd know better by now."

The doctor said they were going to move Suki to a different hospital, a psychiatric hospital, which was for people whose brains weren't working right.

"A psychotic hospital?" My voice shook. "She had a psychotic break?" *Like Mama. She'd disappear like Mama.*

The doctor looked at me. "Psychiatric," she said. "Different word. People who are psychotic have lost touch with reality. That's not your sister. Psychiatric hospitals treat all sorts of mental disorders."

"Suki doesn't have a mental disorder," I said.

Francine put her hands on my shoulders. "Remember when you thought I was calling you crazy?" she said.

"When I was asking your caseworker to get you help? When bad things happen to people, it can mess with their heads. It's not your fault, or Suki's."

"Your sister needs help," the doctor said. "She'll stay in the hospital for a week or two, and then she'll probably have outpatient therapy. We'll take good care of her."

Francine got out her phone. "I'll get one of my friends to give us a ride home."

"Hang on," I said. I took Francine's phone and dialed Teena's number.

We waited in the hallway outside Suki's room. I'd told Teena the room number. Normally it would take at least twenty minutes to drive from Teena's house to the hospital on the far side of town, but Teena and her mom got to us fast.

I couldn't help it. The moment I saw Teena, I started to bawl. Teena put her arms around me and rocked me back and forth. "Shh, shh," Teena said. "Shh, shh."

Teena's mom and Francine looked each other over. "She needed help," Teena's mom said, in an I-don't-know-what-was-wrong-with-you tone. "What Teena told me, she should have been getting all kinds of help. It shouldn't have come to this."

"I agree." Francine ran her hand through her hair. "I been asking for mental health evaluations for weeks," she said. "The state wouldn't pay attention." She sighed. "Even I didn't think she was this bad, and I know all the warning signs. But also, I should have guessed sooner what that snowman did to her."

"You *knew*?" I shouted. I jumped forward, ready to punch her. Teena held me back.

"Not until tonight," Francine said. "Even then—I'm guessing. But I'm right, aren't I? You think so too? That man—he did terrible things to her. For years, probably."

I swallowed. Nodded. Tears dripped off my chin.

Suki was so afraid of Clifton. She hated him so much, even when she pretended as hard as she could that nothing was wrong.

Years.

I'd had sixty seconds of terror. Suki had had years.

Teena's fingers dug into my shoulders. She said, "It's true. I asked her—right before the police came. She didn't say anything, but the way she looked at me I knew the answer."

Teena knew, and Teena's mom knew. "That's why she didn't want to be around you," I said. "That's why she didn't want me around you, either." It wasn't that Teena couldn't keep a secret. It's that she shouldn't keep this one. Probably wouldn't keep this one.

And Suki didn't want anyone to know.

Including me.

Especially me.

Even though she was so lost she stabbed herself with a knife.

Even though she was hurting so bad, she'd do anything to try and stop it.

I understood. It kind of made sense, even though—no. Suki was in a hospital. Suki nearly died. I didn't understand it at all.

For a moment my whole mind blanked out, white and calm and full of nothingness. I took a deep breath. That was easier, but it wasn't real. I shook my head, and the world came back into view.

"We thought she'd told the police," Teena's mom was saying. "That night. We figured she had to. We thought everybody knew the whole story."

Francine shook her head. "Only the part caught in the photograph. That's all they reported."

I said, "Only the part about me."

Teena went into the room to see Suki.

Teena's mom said, "At least now she'll get the help she needs."

"She should have gotten help before this," I said.

"Yep," Francine said. "Someone should have helped both of you. Someone should have paid attention, long time ago."

Teena's mom drove us home. Francine sat up front. I sat in the back with Teena. She put her arm around me just like Suki would have. "Thank you for calling me this morning," she whispered. "Keep calling, okay? Let me know how she's doing. You too."

"It was my fault," I whispered. "She got really mad at me. Last night. She said she had to do everything for me."

Teena pulled me closer. "It wasn't your fault."

"She always had to take care of me."

"Still wasn't your fault."

I felt like it was. When Clifton came after me, Suki'd moved fast to save me. No one had jumped in to save Suki. Including me.

28

At home Francine told me not to step into the kitchen. She said I should go straight to bed. It was daylight. Morning. We'd been up most of the night. Francine said, "Wait. You want some cocoa or something?"

Francine looked more like a pug dog than ever. She was still wearing the flannel pants she slept in, and an old baggy sweatshirt. Her face was all lined and her hair uncombed. It looked almost as ratty as mine on a bad day.

"Why the snow would I want cocoa?"

She shrugged. "Isn't that supposed to be—I don't know—comforting? Or something. Seems like something someone would do. Cocoa."

I thought of how the kitchen would be all over spattered

with Suki's blood. The knife still somewhere on the floor. I thought of walking into that kitchen and heating up a mug of cocoa. Of all things.

I started to laugh.

So did Francine.

"We're way beyond cocoa, aren't we?" she said.

I nodded. My laughs started turning into tears. Francine waved me down the hall, and I climbed up into the top bunk and pressed my face into Suki's pillow. I didn't fall asleep for a long, long time.

When I woke up it was past lunchtime. Saturday. I was alone. I mean, Francine was there, but not Suki.

Even when I spent the night at Nevaeh's, I knew exactly where Suki was: Food City, then Francine's. Now she was somewhere I couldn't picture at all. She could have been on Mars, for all I knew. Memphis. Kansas, with Mama.

Francine called the psychiatric hospital. They said Suki was admitted and safe, but they wouldn't let either of us talk to her. They said they'd started a treatment plan. They said we could come get her in a few days, or maybe a week, or maybe longer. They'd let us know.

Francine and I sat on the couch side by side. Neither of us did anything. Francine had already cleaned up the kitchen. I'd checked. The knife was back in its drawer.

Eventually Francine said, "Want to take a walk?"

"To where?" I said.

Francine shrugged. "It's a pretty fall day."

It was, sure, but I'd never walked just to walk before. But whatever. I put on my shoes.

First Francine drove us, in her car, to a parking lot a few minutes away. I thought we could have just started walking without getting in the car, but then we got out and there was a path, not a road but also not a sidewalk, just dirt beat down firm beside a stream. Trees grew on hills along both sides. Their leaves were all different colors, red and gold and brown, and the air smelled like toast. "See?" Francine said as we walked down the path. "It's a park. It's nice."

"I suppose. Where we headed?"

"Just along here," she said. "When you've had about half of enough, let me know. We'll turn around and go back."

"Really? That's how this works?"

"Yep," she said.

Some people passed us because they were walking faster than us. Other people passed us from the other direction. Some of them had dogs on leashes sniffing the dirt. It was a lot of people doing something I never knew people did.

"Are there any wolves around here?" I asked. I saw a dog that looked like one.

"In this park or in Tennessee?"

"Anywhere around here." We were real close to Virginia.

Francine blew out her breath. "There's some at Bays' Mountain, I think. Used to be. That's a park over by Kingsport."

"How far away is it?"

"Thirty minutes or so. By car."

I thought about that. "Can we go there sometime?"

"If you want to," Francine said. After a while she added, "The wolves are in cages. It's a wolf exhibit. Like at a zoo."

I made a face. "Oh." I didn't want to see wolves in cages. They'd remind me too much of Suki. "I want to see wild wolves."

Francine said, "I think you'd have to go out west to do that."

"Nashville?"

"Montana."

Huh. We'd learned about the fifty states in third grade, but I couldn't remember one single thing about Montana. You'd think I'd remember if they told me Montana had wolves.

I said, "Can we go to Montana?"

"Probably not." Francine didn't sound sorry. "In the summer, though, we'll take a trip to the beach. I go for a week every year."

"Where's the beach?" I knew what a beach was.

"Usually Myrtle. South Carolina. Lots of hotels. Lots of people, lots of restaurants and mini-golf and stuff going on. Ice cream. You'll like it. You ever seen the ocean?"

I shook my head.

Francine said, "It's real nice. I look forward to that week all year."

Francine knew I had started swimming at the Y. Every

school night she reminded me to put my swimsuit in the dryer so it was always dry enough to go back in my backpack the next day.

"I'll get you a new swimsuit, before our beach trip," she said now. "Nothing wrong with the one the Y gave you, but it'll be pretty worn out by then. They stock swimsuits at Walmart in the spring."

"Suki'll need one too," I said.

"We'll get one for Suki," said Francine.

It was strange, because we were talking about everything but Suki hurting herself, when I could hardly think of anything else. The trees and the walk and the idea of a beach were all distracting, nice, but my brain stayed on Suki. Mostly, on Suki with the knife. And Suki yelling. *Do I always have to take care of you?*

And Suki keeping me safe from Clifton. And no one keeping Suki safe at all.

"Can we turn around now?" I asked. "Can we go home?"

"Sure," said Francine.

Next day—Sunday—we went to Food City. Had to. We were out of stuff to eat. Francine had already called and told them Suki wouldn't be in to work that week. She told them that Suki was in the hospital but not that she was in a special hospital for people whose brains were malfunctioning because they'd been hurt so bad they tried to hurt themselves. "It's her story," Francine said, when I asked her why not. "She can tell it however she wants."

I supposed.

Food City wasn't fun on a Sunday. Somebody other than Maybelline was working the deli counter. I couldn't ask a stranger for a free cookie when I knew I was really too old. I didn't see Tony, either. We just bought groceries. We didn't get Suki's employee discount. I didn't get to choose a treat.

"What if they fire her?" I asked as we walked out.

"They might," Francine said. "If they do she can find another job. There's plenty of places hiring." She sighed. "Or, you know, she could just not work for a while."

"She has to work. She's got to save up."

"She doesn't, not really. She could stay in care. You both could."

"Nah," I said.

Except. What if Suki had died? What would have happened to me then?

I needed Suki to sing to me. I needed Suki to hold my hand.

All weekend, at least some of what I felt was happy that Suki was still alive, but by Monday morning the only feelings I had left were terrible. *What if Suki had died? How would I have ever lived without her?* And the persistent voice, like a train rumbling along tracks through the back of my mind: *My fault. My fault. My fault.*

I felt all tight inside. I hadn't slept—couldn't get used to being by myself in the room—and I couldn't believe I had to go to school. I did, though. Francine went to work.

We started off with a spelling test. I'd forgotten about the test—not that I was likely to study for it anyhow—and I don't like spelling on a good day. Ms. Davonte said a word, and I swear I'd never even heard it before, much less knew how to spell it. I stared at my blank paper. I didn't know where to start.

Ms. Davonte said a second word. She walked past my desk, glanced down at my paper, stopped. Tapped the paper. "I expect you to at least try," she said.

I didn't move. I'd numbered the side of my page, one down to twenty. We had eighteen words to go.

Ms. Davonte said a third word.

I mean, I could hear it. My ears worked. But between my ears and my brain was some kind of wall made of Clifton. What he'd done. What it was like, living in his house, afraid all the time. What it was like, knowing I hadn't been nearly afraid enough.

What it had been like for Suki.

Suki with that knife in her hand.

"Della," Ms. Davonte said. She tapped my paper again. "I don't care if you try and fail. I do care if you don't try."

Try. T. R. Y. I could spell that.

Die. D. I. E. Suki. Didn't. Die.

Ms. Davonte stood over me. She said, "I am not moving until you write some words on that piece of paper."

I wrote SNOW.

Only, of course, it wasn't actually *snow*.

SNOW. SNOW. SNOW. SNOW.

29

Ms. Davonte grabbed me by the shoulder and hauled me out into the hall. She said, "You are not fooling me with this stupid act, Della! You have got to do better! You owe it to yourself!"

I rolled my eyes. "What. Ever."

She sent me to the principal's office. Which at least got me out of the spelling test.

The principal—Dr. Penny—said, "Good morning, Della."

"Not really," I said.

This was the first time I'd gotten sent to her office—it was well before all that snow with the family tree—so we didn't know each other yet.

"What brings you here?" she asked.

I shrugged. "Ms. Davonte didn't like the word I wrote on my spelling test."

Dr. Penny asked what word I'd written. I told her. She said, "Did you spell it correctly?"

Which maybe I would have found funny some other time. As it was, I just nodded. Then Dr. Penny said, "Della, what happened?" and I started to cry.

I hated crying and I felt like I'd done nothing but cry and yet there I was again, tears and snot all over my face. Dr. Penny didn't say anything else. She handed me a wad of tissues and told me to sit down in her comfortable chair, and when I was finished crying, suggested I just stay put until I felt calmer. She didn't ask again what was wrong. That was good, because I didn't know how to explain.

I went back to class right before lunch. As soon as Ms. Davonte dismissed us for the cafeteria, Nevaeh grabbed my arm. I jumped, but she held on. "Della," she said, looking right at me, "what happened?"

I didn't cry this time, but I still didn't answer. Out of the corner of my eye, I saw Ms. Davonte lean in, listening. I didn't want her to overhear. I shook my head once, hard. Nevaeh nodded. She didn't say anything else. She got her lunch and sat down next to me, her shoulder almost touching mine. We ate together, in silence. Neither of us said a word.

Nevaeh was my real true friend.

At the end of the day, Ms. Davonte wrote something on a piece of paper and sealed it in an envelope and handed it to me. "Take this to your mother," she said.

I handed it back to her. "Better if you just mail it," I said. "Not that she's going to reply." Ms. Davonte looked at me. "My mother's incarcerated," I said. "In Kansas."

I was sitting at my desk. I probably said it loud enough for half the class to hear. I didn't care. I was past caring.

Ms. Davonte blinked. "I mean, give it to your foster mother," she said. "I'm sorry, Della. I forgot."

I know she had, like, twenty-five kids to teach, but it still didn't seem like something she ought to forget. I mean, it was the second-most important thing about me.

The first-most important thing was Suki.

Ms. Davonte pushed the envelope into my hand. "Tell her I need a reply," she said.

Awesome. Francine was going to be so happy. She'd had a stellar few days from Suki and me.

I went to the Y. I didn't want a snack. I wasn't about to do homework. I didn't want to talk to anyone. I sat down at my usual round table and buried my head in my arms.

Nevaeh sat next to me. She leaned close. She said, "Can you tell me yet?"

It was the *yet* that got me. Like she knew for sure I would tell her eventually. Knew for sure I would trust her.

I lifted my head a few inches. I said, "Suki stuck a knife in her wrist. A big knife. Deep."

Nevaeh's eyes got wide. She whispered, "I'm so sorry." After a minute she whispered, "Did she live?"

I nodded. I put my head back down and didn't lift it up again. I heard Nevaeh say, "Nah, I'm not going to swim today." I heard other noises too, but I ignored them.

Eventually Nevaeh nudged me. "Time to go home," she said.

I sat up. She'd taken crayons and drawn a whole field of flowers on a white sheet of paper, all colors and sizes, blue and red and yellow and purple above a sea of green. She said, "When I'm sad I like to draw happy things," and gave the paper to me.

30

Francine read Ms. Davonte's note, sighed, wadded it up, and threw it away.

"You need to answer that," I said.

She said, "I will."

Francine *phoned* Ms. Davonte. She went into her bedroom and shut the door so I couldn't hear what she was saying, but I could imagine it. Clifton. Foster care. Hospital. Suki's knife and all that blood.

Francine came back into the kitchen. "Cut me up some carrots, will you?"

"No way," I said.

"Yes, way." Francine said. She reached into the drawer and pulled out a smaller knife. "Use this one," she said.

What Suki did with the knife from the drawer. What Clifton did to Suki. What Clifton tried to do to me.

"Take a breath, Della," Francine said. "This is hard, but you'll get through it."

I glared at her. She said, "I mean it. Breathe deep, count to three, let it out."

I breathed deep. She counted. I let it out. "Good," she said. "Do that again."

I did. I felt a little better. "What'd you tell Ms. Davonte?"

Francine said, "That you'd be late to school tomorrow. You've got an appointment with a therapist at eight."

"What for?"

"Whaddaya mean 'what for'? To help you."

I didn't know how it would help. I didn't know how anyone could help who wasn't Suki.

I still wasn't allowed to phone Suki. I asked. Francine was all matter-of-fact about it, but later, at bedtime, she said, "You can sleep out here on the couch if you'd rather. Keep the TV on if you want."

It would probably be better than being alone in the bedroom. I studied Francine. "Did any of your other foster kids ever—"

"That is actually none of your business," Francine said. "I told you before. Their stories are their own."

"But—"

"You and Suki aren't the only kids bad stuff has happened to," Francine said. "I'm sorry. Bad stuff happens all the time."

"You mean bad stuff like Clifton or bad stuff like Mama?"

"Both," Francine said. "I'm sorry."

She tapped her fingers on the arm of the couch. She said, "I told you, nobody goes into foster care for good reasons. Foster care might be better than anything you've ever had in your life so far, and it will still never be as good as what you should have had. If the family you were born into was what it should have been."

I thought about this for a minute. I said, "It was my fault."

"It was not," Francine said. "Don't start down that road."

I was miles down that road. I picked at the edge of my fingernail. I said, "Did bad things ever happen to you?"

Francine took a big breath in, counted three, blew it out slow. She said, "Yes. But that's my story. Not that I won't ever tell you, but it's nothing for you to worry about right now.

"Go to sleep," she said. "I am."

I took Suki's pillow and our blanket out to the couch. I turned the TV on with the volume down low. I turned out the living room lights.

The light from the TV flickered blue across the walls. I watched it. My purple high-tops, that I'd taken off and left by the door, bounced in and out of shadow.

Suki'd bought me the high-tops. She'd used part of her

own clothing allowance. I remember her laughing in Old Navy. I remembered her saying, "Who needs more than two bras?"

In the emergency room they'd cut off the clothes she was wearing. Her shirt and her bra and even her blue jeans. Francine had had to pack up the rest of Suki's clothes and take them to the hospital so she would have something to wear. She only had one bra now.

Would they let her do laundry in the psych hospital?

Do I have to do everything for you?

She had. She'd even bought me those snowflake shoes out of her own clothing allowance, when I couldn't make do with mine.

I took too much from her.

My fault.

I loved my high-tops, but right at that moment I hated them too.

31

In the morning, I still couldn't stand the sight of my high-tops. I went into Suki and my bedroom and dug my old free-clothes-closet shoes out of my dresser's bottom drawer. I shut my high-tops in the drawer instead.

If Francine noticed me wearing my old skank shoes, she didn't say anything.

The therapist's office was in the same building where I'd gone to talk about Clifton into the camera, for the trial. Suki wasn't there. I asked. The therapist's room had white walls and blue chairs, a desk, a couch, and some tables. The therapist wore blue jeans and sandals. No socks. She came into the room with a big yellow dog at her heels. "I'm Dr. Fremont," she said. "This is Rosie, our office dog. Some people like to have her sit with them while they're talking to me. Would you like that?"

I wasn't sure. I didn't know many dogs, mainly just the neighbor's yappy one I never messed with. But Rosie walked up to me, very quietly on great big feet, and put her head next to my knee. She looked me right in the eye. I put my hand on her head, and she sighed and leaned against me.

Sort of like a really friendly soft yellow wolf.

So yeah, she could stay.

Rosie jumped up on the couch and put her huge head into my lap, and I could stroke her and talk at the same time. Though I didn't have to say much. Which was good, because I didn't want to say anything.

"Would you like to talk to me about your sister?" Dr. Fremont asked.

I said, "Absolutely not." I wanted to talk *to* my sister, but nobody was letting me do that.

"Is there anything else you want to talk about right now?"

"Nope," I said. I'd maybe rather be in school than sitting in this office. Even though the office had Rosie instead of Trevor and Ms. Davonte.

In this office, I didn't know any of the rules.

"All right," Dr. Fremont said, not ruffled even a little bit. "What I'd like to do is talk about feelings. How are you feeling right now?"

I had no idea. Zero. Zip. None. I mean, I knew I didn't

want to be sitting there. I knew I didn't feel *good*. Besides that? I shrugged.

Dr. Fremont handed me a piece of paper that had rows of different cartoon faces drawn on it, like little emojis. The faces were labeled: happy, silly, proud, annoyed. She handed me a pen. I looked at the faces and started circling. *Sad, scared, sleepy. Worn-out. Angry. Confused. Disobedient, grief, lonely. Guilt. Strong. Ashamed.*

Dr. Fremont took the paper back. "That's a lot of feelings," she said.

I nodded. Once I'd got to circling, it was hard to stop. Invisible? Worried? On edge? Turned out I was a lot of things.

Dr. Fremont told me she knew about Suki and about Clifton. She'd read a report from Suki's doctor.

"How is she?" I asked.

"She's getting help."

"That doesn't tell me anything."

"She'll get better," Dr. Fremont said. "It will take some time. It always takes time to heal. But for now, you can trust she's somewhere safe."

I did not know whether or not the psych hospital was safe. How could I know? I'd never been there before. Also? If there was a safe place in the world, I probably wouldn't recognize it. Francine's house wasn't safe, not after what happened to Suki there.

Dr. Fremont picked up the paper with the faces I'd circled. "Which of these feelings is the strongest right now?"

Guilt. Ashamed.

"It was my fault," I said. "She had to do too much to take care of me and she didn't want to be around me anymore." I stared at the tips of my skank shoes.

Dr. Fremont set down the paper. "It was not your fault," she said.

"If I'd let—if Suki hadn't—" I didn't mean to, but I squeezed Rosie's ear hard. She let out a soft moan. "I'm sorry," I said to her.

"Rosie likes having her ears rubbed," Dr. Fremont said. "That was a happy moan. Della, none of this is your fault."

"If I—"

"It wasn't your fault."

"But—"

"A lot of kids blame themselves when bad things happen. It isn't true. This wasn't your fault."

I was going to fall apart completely, which I didn't want to do. I sucked in a noisy gulp of air.

"Breathe slow," Dr. Fremont said. "Let it out slow."

I did.

She leaned forward. She looked me in the eye. She said, "None of this was your fault. None of it was Suki's fault. Adults are supposed to take care of children. Neither of you should have been hurt like you were."

It sounded nice, but I couldn't believe it.

"What I think we should do today," Dr. Fremont said, "is work on ways to help you feel better, right now. How to feel more calm."

"Am I allowed to feel better?" I asked. "After Suki—" I didn't know how to finish the sentence. How could I feel better when Suki felt so sad?

"Do you want Suki to feel better?"

Absolutely. I nodded. Dr. Fremont said, "Maybe she already does. At the hospital, they'll be helping her feel better. She'd want the same for you."

We practiced belly breathing again, sucking air in slowly, down, down, down, until I could feel my belly stretching round like a balloon. Then slowly pushing all the air out, my belly limp and flat. Then breathing in, in, in. Then out, out, out. "Francine already had me do this," I said.

"Good," Dr. Fremont said. "Did it help?"

"How would I know?"

"If you felt calmer afterward," she said, "it helped."

"Oh. Then yeah, I guess so."

We worked on making lists: five things I could see, four things I could feel. Three things I could hear, two I could smell, one I could taste. I bent my head down to Rosie's neck. "I smell dog," I said. "It smells kind of funky, but not awful. But I don't taste anything." Was my spit supposed to taste like something?

"Here." Dr. Fremont handed me a peppermint, sharp and sweet.

She gave me more things to try: counting backwards from 100 by 7s. Spelling my name backwards. "You do know my full name's Delicious, don't you?" I asked.

"Actually, I didn't," she said. "That presents a challenge."

I had to shut my eyes before I could do it. "S-U-O-I-C-I-L-E-D."

Dr. Fremont applauded. "And can you tell how much more relaxed you are than when you first came in?"

I could. My stomach muscles didn't hurt. My skin didn't feel itchy.

"Great," she said. "Now let's come up with a list of things you like to do. Things that make you feel happy. Things you can do every day."

I liked to eat Cheetos. I liked to be with Suki.

"Your sister loves you so much," Dr. Fremont said. "But she can't heal you. Only you can do that. Plus, what you enjoy is probably different from what Suki enjoys."

I didn't know whether or not that was true. I hadn't spent much time thinking about what I liked, and I didn't really know what Suki liked, either. I mean, Cherry Dr Pepper, sure. Pepperoni on her pizza. Beyond that?

There had to be things beyond that. We'd never looked for them, Suki and me.

I said, "I want to go to Montana."

"Ah," Dr. Fremont said. "That's good. Why Montana?"

I said, "Wolves."

She said I should start planning a trip to Montana. I could look things up and write them down. Where would I go to find wolves? How would I get there? Car or airplane? How long would it take? Where would I stay?

"I can't go to Montana," I said. "It's farther away than Kansas."

Dr. Fremont looked up. "What's in Kansas?"

"Mama."

She shuffled some papers around and said she understood that my mother was incarcerated. She asked if I wanted to talk about that.

I said, "Nope."

She said, "You're allowed to have dreams, Della. You and Suki both."

"Suki has nightmares."

"I mean plans for the future," she said.

I nodded. "I know." I just didn't, that was all.

"Keep going with the wolves," Dr. Fremont said. "That sounded like something."

I nodded. "I was raised by a wolf," I said.

When I got to school Ms. Davonte had rearranged all the desks. Trevor was way in the back, near where Ms. Davonte had moved her own desk. I was in the middle of the room. I didn't sit near Nevaeh anymore—she was off to one side. I sat next to a girl named Mackinleigh, who seemed nice enough. Luisa was only two desks way.

Nobody said anything about my coming in late, and the day went mostly like usual until we were lining up to go to lunch. Then Ms. Davonte pulled me aside. "Della, I was sorry to learn about the trouble with your sister," she said, "and everything else you've been through. Why didn't you tell me, yesterday? Before the spelling test?"

What? Shoo, like I was going to trust her with my business.

Ms. Davonte was still talking. I pulled away, hurried down the hall toward Nevaeh and lunch. Meanwhile I spelled it out in my head, S-U-O-I-C-I-L-E-D D-N-A I-K-U-S.

Dr. Fremont was right. It did help.

32

That night at home I said to Francine, "I need to learn how to make good mac 'n' cheese. And do all the laundry. And everything."

Francine said, "Knock yourself out," and sat down on the couch.

The mac 'n' cheese turned out better than the time before. The laundry turned out fine. At bedtime I curled up on the couch again and watched one of the shopping channels with the sound off. For hours.

Wednesday on the way to the Y, I said to Nevaeh, "I don't want to swim today. I want to play basketball." I missed basketball. Also, I really wanted to sweat. You don't sweat in a swimming pool.

"Okay," Nevaeh said. "Do you want me to play with you or stay outta your way?"

"With," I said, so she did.

Coach Tony was there. I figured he would be. I grabbed a ball right away and started dribbling, running up and down the court as hard as I could without completely losing the ball. Nevaeh tried to match me but couldn't keep up. I was some kind of running machine.

"Della." Coach Tony's voice. I pulled up and turned around. Sweat was already popping out on my forehead and in between my shoulder blades. It felt excellent. My heart was pounding from running, not from being afraid.

"How's your sister?" Coach Tony asked. His face was kind. Concerned. "I heard she was in the hospital."

"She's having a really hard time," I said.

He nodded. "I'm sorry."

He said it like he meant it.

"It's a psychiatric hospital," I said. "She's having mental health problems."

I don't know what made me say that.

Tony flinched a little. "I'm sorry," he said again. I waited for him to say something else, but he didn't.

"Can she still work for you?" I asked him.

He nodded again. "Once she's better," he said. "When she's feeling well enough, we'll put her back on the schedule. You can tell her that, if you want to."

Then he blew his whistle to call all the basketball players together. He started us off on his favorite passing drill. After that we worked on layups. Nevaeh was better at basketball than I expected. "I played on the rec team last year," she said. "Here at the Y, on Saturdays. In the winter. It was fun. We could both do it this winter, if you want to."

"Nah," I said.

"Why not? You said you like basketball."

I couldn't do things like that. Where Francine would have to sign me up, and pay extra, and drive me back and forth. Suki and me, we'd been trouble enough already. "Nah."

I didn't get to talk to Suki on Wednesday, or Thursday. I survived the entire week without once talking to my sister. Then it was Friday, the hardest day, and I got through that too. When Francine picked me up at the Y, she tossed me a bag of fast food. "Dinner on the way," she said. "We're going to go see Suki."

The hospital smelled like a school, not a place for sick people. It was a low building stuck behind trees. The hallway walls were painted soft puke green. There were two sets of doors. The second one was locked. Francine spoke into an intercom and someone let us in.

We went into a room with a big table in it and there was Suki, sitting in a chair in the corner, her legs folded under her like always. When she saw me she made a little noise, like a startled baby. I dove at her and she hugged me and hugged me and we both sobbed.

I don't know why I was crying. I don't cry much. I never used to cry.

I don't know why Suki was crying, either, but a tiny part of me was glad she was. Glad she missed me, a little at least.

After a minute or two, Francine said, "Sit down next to Suki, Della. Her doctor is here to talk with us."

I scooted my chair right next to Suki's. I reached out to grab her hand, but missed and caught her by the wrist. The hurt wrist, the one with all the stitches. She gasped in pain. I jumped back. She reached around with her other hand and clutched mine.

We didn't talk. We didn't move.

The doctors and some other people and Francine discussed Suki's treatment and how well she was doing, which was medium well. Not hurting herself again but not ready to come home. At least another week in the hospital. At least another week away from me.

When they finally quit talking, Francine said, "We'll give you two a few minutes alone."

Suki's doctor said, "Only a few minutes. Suki, we'll be right outside." Like maybe I was going to cause trouble for Suki.

Suki covered her face in her hands. The cuff of her sweat-shirt pulled back and I could see the neat row of stitches running down the line in her wrist. She uncovered her face.

Her eyes were full of tears. She leaned forward and asked, "Are you mad at me?"

Suddenly I was. I really, really was. I stood up and said, "You ever try anything like that again, I'm gonna kill you."

She gave a tiny snort of laughter. "Well—"

"It's not funny!" I said. "It wasn't funny! It was worse than Clifton!"

Her smile evaporated. Her eyes flashed fire. "Was not," she said.

"Was," I insisted. "Clifton, he's over. If you'd died it would have been forever."

"I don't feel like I'll ever be over him," she said.

"That doesn't mean you won't be."

"That's what my therapist says," Suki said. "I dunno if I believe him."

She looked so frail and scared and I still felt like punching her. "I've got a therapist too," I said. "She has a dog that reminds me of you. Of a wolf."

Suki bit her lips. "Raised by wolves," she whispered. "I swear, I was doing my best."

I said, "I *like* being raised by a wolf. Wolves live in packs. They take care of each other."

"Wild animals," Suki said.

Yes. "They fight back, Suki. Nothing kills a wolf."

She lifted one shoulder. "How do you know?"

I didn't. But I could imagine.

Francine cracked open the door. "Della," she said. "Time's up." She handed Suki a plastic bag. "Here. Brought you more bras and underwear. Socks. A couple new T-shirts."

"Thanks," Suki said. "You showed my doctors?"

Francine nodded. I was confused, until Suki said, "I can only have what they say I can have. Things they've checked out, that I can't use to hurt myself."

"Can you have a phone? Can I call you?"

She shook her head. "Not yet. Soon. I hope." She gave me a kiss. "Be tough."

I didn't answer.

On the drive home, I wished I had another paper like the one Dr. Fremont gave me, with all the emotions on it. I tried to work out how I felt. Angry, mostly. Also sad. I kicked the car's dashboard until Francine made me stop.

"Why'd you bring Suki clothes?" I asked. "Where'd you get them?"

"Went shopping on my lunch hour," Francine said. "She needed them. I told you, I've got to provide the two of you with the stuff you need."

"Yeah? Well, I need my sister back."

"I know," Francine said. "I'm only responsible for the *stuff*, Della. Suki's responsible for Suki. I can't help that."

I practiced my belly breathing. I spelled names backwards in my head. Della and Suki and Francine. E-N-I-C-N-A-R-F. I was still angry.

"Who's responsible for *me*?" I asked.

"I am," Francine said. "Same as I'm responsible for Suki."

"But you just said—"

"You know what I mean," she said. "I'm responsible for getting you and Suki the things you need. For your food and shelter and care. You're responsible for what you say and do."

"Who's responsible for loving me?"

I didn't mean to say it. Didn't know I was going to.

We had just pulled into Francine's driveway. The porch light was out and the windows were dark and cold. Francine turned off the car's ignition. She sat silently for a moment.

"Suki loves you, and you love Suki," Francine said. "You're lucky. You have each other. As you get older, you'll find more people to love you and to love."

"She loves me but she almost left me," I said.

"She loves you, and she didn't want to leave you," Francine said. "Someone hurt her bad enough that she almost couldn't bear the pain. But she can. She's getting help. She'll hurt less. Her life will get better and better. So will yours."

I looked at her. In the weird dark shadows, the bumps on her face stuck out more than ever. If I put a pointy black hat on her, she'd look exactly like a witch. "How do you know?" I whispered.

"I know," Francine said. "I been around the block a few times." She grabbed my arm. "Clifton's in the past," she said. "He's over. Leave him there. Don't let him wreck your future too."

33

Clifton might have been in my past, but Trevor was in my present. On Monday he pinched me on the playground. Right in the middle of my back, the way he pinched all the girls. "Baby!" he said.

I whirled around and punched him in the gut. Hard. Nobody saw the pinch, but teachers saw the punch, especially since Trevor hollered and nearly burst into tears. The slime-faced snowman.

It became this whole big deal. Apparently punching people is a lot worse than pinching them, or even calling them snowmen.

In the office, Ms. Davonte and Dr. Penny got out the

student handbook and showed me where punching Trevor was very much against the rules.

"He pinched me first," I said. "Where's that in the rules?"

"It was an accident!" Trevor said.

"He pinched me right where—"

"He's not allowed to pinch you," Dr. Penny said.

"Accident," Trevor repeated again. "Like her tripping me was an accident."

"But punching him escalates the situation," Dr. Penny continued. "If someone does something to you, you need to tell a teacher, Della."

Ms. Davonte put on a pity-look. "I know you're having some trouble at home right now, but that doesn't excuse your behavior."

See? Like I'd tell her anything. She wasn't someone I could trust. I said, "I didn't punch Trevor because of my sister."

Dr. Penny said, "Physical violence is never appropriate."

Wasn't pinching me physical violence? Also the bra-strap thing—it was creepy in a Clifton kind of way. "I'm not sorry I hit him," I said. "If I had it to do over again, I'd hit him harder."

Dr. Penny exchanged a look with Ms. Davonte. I got in-school suspension. That meant I had to sit and do worksheets in a corner of the library all the rest of the day. Classes came in and out of the library. Once in a while the librarian came over to check on me, but mostly she left me alone with my thoughts, and that wasn't good.

I kept thinking about Suki.

And Clifton.

And what Clifton did to Suki.

And Mama.

And everything Mama didn't do.

Couldn't do.

Would never do.

And how much I missed her, even though I never really knew her at all. How much Suki had to miss Mama.

How Mama left us with Clifton. Maybe not on purpose, but she still did.

Besides Trevor, I've only ever punched one kid. It was the year Suki and I were at the same school together, so it must have been just after Mama got arrested, when we were first with Clifton and I was in kindergarten. Suki and me had recess at the same time. I don't remember why I punched the other kid, but I did. The kid ran off crying to the teacher, and I went and hid behind my sister. When the teacher came up to chew me out, Suki said, "Della didn't hit him. I did."

The kid knew that wasn't true but he must have been afraid of Suki or something, because he didn't say another word.

Suki got in trouble. I felt bad, but Suki just shook her head at me, and afterward, at home, said, "I'm tough, Della. I can take it. I don't mind."

She took too much.

I minded.

I sat in the corner of the library and practiced my belly breathing. I saw five things and heard four and smelled nineteen or whatever. It didn't help. I still minded. I was still so sad for my sister.

I didn't finish the stupid worksheets, but there was no way I was doing homework at the Y. When we got there I went straight to the gym. I got out a ball and started running up and down the floor.

"Hey!" Nevaeh stuck her head into the gym. "Are you mad at me?"

I grabbed the ball. "No," I said. "Course not. Why?"

"You didn't sit with me on the bus. And now you're not even having a snack."

Honestly, the snacks at the Y were not all that great. "I wasn't thinking about you on the bus," I said. I'd sat down in the very first seat, across the aisle from Trevor, who ignored me even though I glared at him. "I'm sorry. I just wanted to get away from school. I was all pent up today. I felt like I might punch somebody else."

I bounced a pass to her. She caught it, awkwardly. I said, "Running helps. Sweating helps. When I'm moving enough to sweat, I don't feel as much like punching someone."

Nevaeh said, "I'm sorry Trevor did that. I'm sorry you got in trouble."

"You told me to keep quiet about it," I said. "Maybe that would have been better than punching him."

"I don't know," Nevaeh said. "I told my mom what you

said, the last time he pinched me. She said maybe you were right. Maybe ignoring him was sort of like giving him permission. I don't want to do that. So I don't know what the right thing is."

"I got in trouble."

"Yeah, but maybe now he'll quit bothering you. Ignoring him didn't make it stop, and neither did telling the teachers."

"I yelled at him before. This was the first time he actually pinched me."

"And this time you hurt him back, didn't you? You punched him. So maybe—"

I saw what Nevaeh meant, and I still wasn't at all sorry I'd hit Trevor, but I knew punching people wasn't a solid long-term solution. For starters, there were probably a lot of people who could hit back harder than me.

I'd never have punched Clifton, for instance. I wouldn't have dared.

It was the photograph Suki took that stopped him. The evidence.

Nevaeh and I ran and shot baskets. Coach showed up and organized us all into drills again. I stayed as far away from Trevor as I possibly could, but one time he ran right up to me. "Hey, baby," he said, grinning, "how'd you like getting suspended?"

"Why would my being suspended make you happy?" I asked. I honestly didn't know.

He laughed and ran away.

■ ■ ■

I didn't tell Francine about the in-school suspension, but when we got home, there was a voicemail about it on her machine.

Francine listened to it and stared at me.

My heart sped up. My breath came short. I thought about which cartoon face I'd circle.

Panic.

"Relax, Della," Francine said. She deleted the message. "I'm not in the mood for cooking tonight. Want to get pizza?" She looked at me. "Why are you this upset? You've been in trouble, like, every week that you've been here."

Exactly. "You said—you said when we got here that if we caused trouble we'd have to find a new place to live."

"*Caused* trouble," Francine said. "Not *had* trouble."

"What's the difference?" I asked.

"Set fire to my house on purpose, that'd be causing trouble," she said. "Slash my furniture. Pee on the carpet—"

"*Pee on the carpet?*"

She flapped a hand. "It happened."

I said, "What if I cooked meth and blew up your bathroom?"

Francine's grin faded. "What?"

"What if I did that? What if I cared more about meth than about my two little girls? What if I let them get stuck in a horrible place where they'd be bad hurt by bad people and no one paid attention or helped them at all? What if I was *that bad?*"

Francine stared at me for what felt like a long, long time. "Then you'd be someone else," she said at last. "First of all, you're not addicted to drugs, and I see no reason why you ever should be. But also, the person you are would never do such a thing. The person you are is tough and resilient and loving and kind."

If that was true, there was only one reason for it. "Because I had Suki."

She nodded. "You were lucky."

"And Suki had nobody."

"That's not true," Francine said. "Suki had you."

"I couldn't fix things. I didn't stop Clifton. I didn't even realize what he was doing to her."

"You didn't know about Clifton," Francine said. "It wasn't your job to stop him."

"I wish I'd known. I wish I'd stopped him."

"Of course," Francine said. "But you love Suki. She's always had that. It's a lot, believe me."

Forget the pizza. For dinner, Francine made us perfect mac 'n' cheese.

Not that I could finish mine. I was too worried about Suki. And me.

34

Next day was therapy, which was awesome because it meant I got to go to school late. I sat down on the couch next to Rosie and I don't know why, I just started talking, about Trevor, about the in-school suspension, about what I'd said to Francine. About Mama.

Dr. Fremont listened. When I finished talking she said, "You want to know why Trevor's bullying you? And why your mama couldn't shake her addiction?"

I nodded. "And why Clifton—why he did what he did."

"I don't know why," Dr. Fremont said. "If I knew their whole stories I might be able to guess, but it would only be a guess." She sat up straighter. "Some people get hurt so badly they lash out. They hurt other people. A small percentage are truly evil. Bad from the start. Addiction is very complicated—some people can shake it off, others never do. I don't know what went wrong with your mama. You'll probably never be able to find out."

Dr. Fremont said, "What Clifton did to you and Suki—that's common."

I jerked my head up so fast that Rosie, who was half asleep across my lap, startled. She licked me once across the face before she lay back down. "*Common?*" My stomach lurched. "You mean—not just Suki and me?"

"Honestly?" Dr. Fremont said. "You're probably not the only kid it's happened to in your class."

I thought for a moment. "You mean in my school, right?" I said. "My class, that's only, like, twenty-five people. Only thirteen girls."

Dr. Fremont looked sad. "I mean in your class. Yes. It happens that often. And it happens to both boys and girls."

It was so icky, so dark in my memory. I had thought it'd had to be just me—me and Suki. Nobody else. "I never heard anything like that," I said. "Nobody ever talks about it."

"I know," she said. "Maybe more people should. Maybe if more people felt they could talk about it, it wouldn't happen as often."

"Does it always cause problems?" I asked.

Dr. Fremont nodded. "Always," she said. "It hurts peo-

200

ple in lots of big ways." She reached out. I thought she was going to pat my arm, and I didn't want her to, but she scratched Rosie's head instead. "The good news is, people can and do heal. They can and do get better."

35

Suki could get better. I was going to hold on to that. I could get better too.

At recess I walked up to Trevor.

"Hey, dummy," he said. "How was suspension?"

I ignored that. "You are not ever allowed to touch me," I said. "You are never, ever allowed to touch me without my permission in any way. So don't."

Dr. Fremont and I had talked about that at the end of our visit. It was called *consent*.

He laughed. "'Without my permission,'" he said. "Hey, dummy. Nobody's going to ask your permission!"

I walked away. What I said wouldn't stop him, probably, but at least I'd said it.

I found Nevaeh and Luisa and Mackinleigh. "I don't have to let him touch me," I explained. Dr. Fremont had said so. "Not ever. You don't either."

Luisa ran her fingers through her braids. She said, "I wish he couldn't touch me without permission. I hate it."

"He *can't*," I said. "He isn't allowed to. That's the rules. For everyone."

Luisa rolled her eyes. "Says who?"

"Everybody," I said.

"Sure," she said. "We'll see how that works."

The next night, Francine and I got to go see Suki again. She wasn't doing as well as her doctors had hoped. Her team said she was struggling. They made me wait in the hallway while they discussed the details with Francine, even though Suki told them I could stay. For a moment, Suki started to insist that I stay, but Francine cut her off. "It's hard on her, Suki," she said. "There are things she doesn't need to know."

"If Suki needs me—" I said.

Francine pushed me out into the hallway. "She needs you to love her. She doesn't need you to be burdened with every detail."

I tried to understand exactly what that meant, but mostly it was this: Suki'd be staying in the hospital for at least another week.

When they were done with their big group meeting they let me talk to her for a few minutes. "What's wrong?" I asked.

"I need to find an acceptable outlet for my pain," Suki said.

"Where'd you learn that?" It didn't sound like something she'd say.

She flapped her hand. "Oh, you know, this place." She said, "I'm trying hard to get better, Della. But it isn't easy."

I asked her, "Did you know it wasn't just us?"

"Whaddya mean?"

"Clifton stuff happens to lots of kids. That's what my therapist says."

"Yeah." Suki's voice was barely above a whisper. "I didn't know that either, until I got here. I thought it was mostly just me. But it happened to a bunch of the kids in here. What Clifton did or something like it. Messed them up. Messed up all of us."

"You need to tell," I said. "Suki. Tell people what Clifton did. He'd stay in prison longer. It'd be safer for everybody."

Suki's face froze. Reminded me of the way she looked when she was staring at the knife. "I've told everybody here," she said. "The doctors know. My therapist knows. That means the police have to know too. Doctors and therapists are mandatory reporters."

I blew out a big breath. "That's great."

"That doesn't mean I'm going to press charges," Suki said. "I'm not."

I said, "You're going to let Clifton get away with it."

"He's not getting away with it," Suki said. Her eyes

flashed and she sounded angry again. "We're taking him to court for what he did to you. We have evidence. He won't be able to talk his way out of that photo. It's easy."

"Is not—" I said, remembering the tight feeling in my stomach the day I made the tape. How scared I felt.

"Easier," she corrected. "We don't have photographs of what he did to me. It'd be my word against his. I'd have to sit in the courtroom while his lawyers tried to make it sound like I was lying. I'd have to sit in front of him—I'd have to look at him—and I can't do it, Della. I'm sorry. The people here, they promised they wouldn't make me."

"You're stronger than that," I whispered.

She laughed and gestured to the walls. "Current evidence suggests otherwise."

It was hard to disagree with the soft puke walls of a psych hospital. Which didn't mean I didn't want to try.

I wanted to climb into Suki's lap, or pull her into mine. Instead I said, "Tell me something good about Mama."

"What?"

"I mostly only remember the motel," I said. "Can you remember anything good? Tell me one good thing."

Suki reached across the space between our chairs. She wrapped her arms around me. She put her chin on the top of my head. "Hmm," she said. "Oh, yeah. I've got one." For the first time that night, she smiled. "Right after you were born, I went to go see you in the hospital. I'd been staying with some of Mama's friends and they brought me in. Mama was in this big bed with white sheets, her head propped up, holding you. You were wrapped in a blanket and had a pink hat on your head."

"What did I look like?"

"All I could see was your little squished face," Suki said. "I climbed up on the bed and Mama put her arm around me. She said, 'Here's your new sister.' I leaned over to get a better look, and you scrunched your eyes up and started to scream.

"And Mama laughed," Suki said. "She said, 'We know how to make her feel better, don't we, Suki?' And she started singing. 'Skinna-ma-rinky-dinky-dink. Skinna-ma-rinky-do. I love you.'"

"She sang that?" I said. "I thought it came from Teena's mom's tape."

"It was on Teena's mom's tape," Suki said. "Mama sang it to us first. Long time ago."

She scooped me closer, leaned her cheek against mine. We sang together.

Skinnamarinky dinky dink, skinnamarinky do,
I love you.
Skinnamarinky dinky dink, skinnamarinky do,
I love you.
I love you in the morning, and in the afternoon.
I love you in the evening, underneath the moon.
Skinnamarinky dinky dink, skinnamarinky do,
I love you.

Suki and me, we loved each other. Once upon a time, our mama loved us too.

"Oh, Della," Suki said, "why are you wearing those horrible shoes?"

I stretched my feet out. They *were* horrible shoes. "I don't know," I said. "I felt like I took too much from you. I took your money for the purple shoes."

She shook her head at me. "I wanted to buy you the purple shoes. They're fantastic. Also, you give me more than you take."

I didn't know about that.

"Also?" Suki said. "Those free-clothes-closet shoes suck."

36

I put my purple shoes back on my feet, and my crummy shoes back in my drawer. That Friday night, Teena came to spend the evening with me while Francine went out to O'Maillin's with her friends.

It was not babysitting. Teena said so. "Like I'd expect to be paid for hanging out with you," she said. "I'm so glad to be here."

"What about your boyfriend?" I asked.

"Ditched him," she said.

First we went to Food City, just for fun. In the deli, Maybelline stuck her hand over the counter when she saw me. Empty, not holding a cookie. It took me a moment to understand what she meant. I stuck my hand out, and she squeezed it.

"How you doing, sugar?" she asked.

I took a breath. "My sister—"

"Not your sister," Maybelline said. "I hope she's well, but I'm asking about you."

"I'm—I don't know. I'm okay. I miss Suki bad."

Maybelline nodded. "Tony said you were having a hard time." She reached into the display case for a chocolate chip cookie.

I said, "Can I have peanut butter instead?" I nodded toward Teena. "Peanut butter's her favorite."

Maybelline smiled. "Sure. It's good to share your cookies with friends."

Francine had given Teena ten bucks to buy snacks. We had a hard time deciding. A grocery store is full of riches when you've got money to spend. I showed her Suki's garlic cheese. She shuddered. I suggested we get some Mountain Dew.

"Girl, that stuff turns your teeth green!" Teena said.

"Does not—"

"It'll probably make you glow in the dark! Nothing that color is meant to go inside your mouth."

In the end we got a box of frozen egg rolls. Teena swore I'd like them. And two donuts with googly frosting eyes and cookies stuffed into their center holes, so they looked like

Muppets. And then, because we still had money left, we each spent fifty cents trying to win stuffed animals in the grab-it game in the lobby. Didn't win, but it was fun trying.

Back at Francine's, Teena stuck the egg rolls in the oven. We ate the donuts at the kitchen table along with some soda from the refrigerator. I told Teena Suki wasn't doing so good.

"She was in pretty bad shape," Teena said. "Broken bones take a long time to heal. Why shouldn't brains?"

Put that way, it made sense. "She's taking medicine now, to help."

Teena clinked her glass against mine. "Hallelujah," she said.

I would have stayed up until Francine got home, but around ten o'clock I started falling asleep on the couch. The third time Teena had to wake me up, she said, "Kiddo, go to bed." She tucked me into the bottom bunk.

"Sing 'Skinnamarinky,'" I said, and she did.

Teena was the only person besides Suki allowed to sing me that song.

In the morning, Francine was sipping her coffee when I walked into the kitchen. Fat-free full-sugar French vanilla creamer. I poured myself a cup, two-thirds coffee and one-third creamer. I took a great big gulp. French vanilla slammed my taste buds. I spat the whole mouthful into the sink. I said to Francine, "You *drink* that? On purpose?"

"You're not supposed to use half the bottle of creamer,"

Francine said. "That sounds bad even to me. You girls have a good time?"

"Yeah," I said. "We saved you an egg roll."

I got it out of the fridge. Francine took a bite. "Thanks," she said.

"Thanks for Teena," I said.

I was sleeping better again, but sometimes, when the headlights of cars turning into the street near us flooded the room with light, it reminded me of the headlights from Clifton's truck cab pulling into the drive. Then I'd remember Suki's panic, and I'd start to panic too. I'd remember the way she'd fold in on herself. My heart would start racing and my breath would come tight.

SOUICILED.

IKUS.

ANEET.

ENICNARF.

HEAVEN.

Nothing I did seemed to help.

We'd heard from one of our lawyers that the trial date was edging closer. We didn't have to do anything about it, she just wanted us to know.

Clifton was in jail for what he did to me.

But not for what he did to Suki.

"How much time would Clifton get for what he did to Suki?" I asked Francine. "I mean, if the police knew everything?"

"Dunno," she said. "It would depend on the details. What exactly he did, and how often, and for how long."

Shoo.

"But more time, right?"

"Absolutely," she said. "At the very least, he'd be a repeat offender." She gave me some side-eye. "You stay out of it. What he did to Suki is Suki's story. Not yours. She gets to make her own choices."

"I think she needs to tell them."

"Not your decision," said Francine.

I said, "When he gets out of prison, he might hurt someone else. Some other little girl. Or girls. The longer he's in prison, the fewer people he can hurt."

"That's true," Francine said.

I said, "Did you know grown-up wolves have no natural predators?" I'd been reading all I could about wolves. The school library didn't have much. Bunch of broken-down old books, and I couldn't find anything about wolves in the books for sale at Walmart. But still, I read what I could.

"Makes sense," said Francine.

"It's true," I said. "Bears and cougars might attack baby wolves, but once they're grown up nothing can stop them."

Francine made an *mmmm* noise, pretending to be listening. I thought it was important. Suki and me, once we grew all the way up, nothing could take us down.

37

"What I want to know," I said to Dr. Fremont, "is how bad things happening to people can actually hurt their brains."

I'd been thinking about it. Brains were shut up inside the hard bone-box that was your skull. If someone or something banged you upside the head, stands to reason your brain could be hurt. But just someone scaring you? Touching you where they shouldn't?

"It's complicated," Dr. Fremont said, "but it's true."

She said that when bad things happened to people, it could make their brains change for the worse. "Especially if the bad things happen when you're young," she said. "Or helpless, or trapped, or if the bad things go on for a long time. Your brain gets more sensitive. Jumpier. Your heart beats faster. You get upset or angry or sad more easily."

She handed me a list of ten ways bad things could happen to a kid. Like, mom in prison. Mom on meth. Not knowing who or what or where your father was. People putting their hand down your pants. All the stuff that had happened to Suki and me. Whew. I mean, we'd never starved. Not that I remembered. Though who knew, back in the day. There's so much I don't remember well. Probably there were days Mama forgot to feed us.

Dr. Fremont nodded when I said so. She said, "Over two-thirds of all children have had at least one of these bad things happen to them."

I had to think about that for a moment. Then I said, "You mean one-third of all kids haven't had any? *None?*"

Dr. Fremont looked startled, but she nodded.

"Wow," I said. I tried to imagine that. I tried to imagine any one of the kids I knew—me, Suki, Teena, Nevaeh, Luisa—any of the kids at my school growing up in some kind of perfect place, without a divorce or being hungry or being hit or any single big thing going wrong. I tried to imagine what it would be like. A perfect life.

Nope. Couldn't do it. Not the kids I knew.

"I've got, like, all ten," I said. "So I'm pretty much screwed?"

Dr. Fremont leaned forward. She smiled. "No," she said.

"This is the important part, Della. *No one is ever screwed.* Not you. Not Suki. Not anyone.

"Bad things happening to you caused bad changes to your brain," Dr. Fremont said. "But brains can change *back.* They heal. Your brain can get better. You can do things to help."

"Really?"

"That's what we're working on here," she said. "Changing your brain. Calming it down."

I'd be calmer if I knew Clifton was staying in prison until I was grown. I thought Suki would be too. I said so.

Dr. Fremont said, "Some things are not entirely within your control."

Sure. But that didn't mean I couldn't control them a little.

Be in charge of my own life. That sounded good.

Wednesday at the Y was a basketball day. Nevaeh and I had decided to take turns, basketball one day, swimming the next. Sometimes Luisa played basketball with us too, even though she liked swimming better.

Trevor'd been leaving me alone since I punched him, but halfway through our session, when we'd moved on from drills to playing half-court scrimmages, he came up to me, reached out one finger, poked me, and said, "Touch."

I stopped dead on the court. "Trevor," I said loudly, "you do not have permission to touch me. Ever."

He laughed.

Coach was on the other half-court, demonstrating boxing out for the three hundredth time.

"Coach," I yelled, "Trevor touched me without my permission."

Coach blew his whistle to restart the other scrimmage and walked to my half-court. "Physical contact is part of playing basketball," he said. "Every touch is not necessarily a foul."

"That isn't what I mean," I said. "He poked me with his finger."

Coach looked at Trevor.

"Joke," Trevor said.

"It wasn't funny," I said. "I'd told him before not to touch me."

Coach blew his whistle. "Trevor, three laps," he said. Then he stood watching while Trevor ran laps and the rest of us started playing again. And yeah, I knew what Coach meant. When this kid named Demetrious boxed out correctly, under the basket, he stuck his whole backside right against my legs and shoved me out of the box, and that was just basketball, that was how you played.

Trevor poking me, much less pinching me, that wasn't a game.

Next day, when Francine picked me up at the Y, she said there was a surprise waiting for me at home. She was grinning big, and I knew what I hoped it was, and I was right.

Suki. Home.

She was sitting on the front step. When the car pulled in, she got to her feet, and she was smiling like the old Suki, bright as the sun. I threw open the door and leaped into her arms.

38

I had a million questions for Suki. She had almost a million answers.

Yes, she would be seeing her therapist still. Three times a week, to start.

Yes, she was taking her medicine.

Yes, it was helping. She liked it.

Yes, she would be going back to school, starting Monday. The school had a plan for getting her caught up.

Yes, she was going to keep working at Food City. She'd call the office in the morning.

Yes, she'd try to get the Friday night shifts again. And I could go with her and help Maybelline.

I asked, "Do you absolutely swear you'll never try anything like that again?"

I waited for her to say yes, but she didn't. Her smile faltered. She said, "I absolutely swear I will always do my best."

"Snow," I said. "That's not good enough, Suki."

Her eyes looked panicky again. She said, "It's all I've got."

"No! I need you to promise!"

"Yo," Francine said to me. "Knock it off. She can't do better than her best."

I swallowed hard. I said, "I really need you to promise, Suki."

Suki thought a moment. "I promise I'll ask for help if things get bad. Okay? I can promise that."

It wasn't enough.

I waited until we were both in bed that night, snug in the top bunk, to ask my last question. "Suki," I said, my voice breaking a little, "did you let Clifton hurt you so he wouldn't hurt me?"

She grabbed my face tight between her hands. "No," she said, in a voice so fierce it was almost a growl. "*No*. I didn't. It was never—I never had any kind of a choice, not that I knew of. He didn't mess with you, that's all." She smoothed my hair. She kissed me. "I'm so glad he didn't. Don't you dare feel guilty."

"How old were you?" I asked. "The first time—"

She knew what I meant. "Eight? Nine? Right after we moved in with him."

I said, "When we still had Mama."

Suki nodded.

I wanted to wail right then. I wanted to howl and scream. Mama had been there. She should have kept Suki safe. She should have protected both of us.

That right there is another of the really hard things.

Suki shrugged. "I'm pretty angry about it. But I don't know whether to be most angry at Mama or the meth or what."

I said, "Clifton."

She said, "Oh, absolutely. I mean besides him."

I said, "We'd be safer if he stayed a long time in prison."

Suki didn't say anything.

I said, "The whole world would be safer if he did."

"Maybe," she said.

"You know it," I said.

She said, "Quit pushing me, Della. I'm doing the best I can."

The next afternoon I went to the Y like always. When Francine and I got home, Suki was sprawled across the top bunk, writing in a notebook she'd brought home from the hospital. It was big and thick, with hard cardboard covers she'd decorated all over with markers. She had her own pack of markers, fancy new ones, and a dark black pen.

"This is my private journal," she said, when I came in. She was writing with the purple marker, scribbling words fast all down one page. Had about half the notebook full of words. "I don't want you reading it, okay? It's just mine. I already told Francine."

Suki used to write in spiral-bound notebooks Clifton bought at the grocery store. Every time she filled a page she ripped it out, wadded it up, and threw it away. I never read anything she wrote.

"Whatever," I said. You'd think I'd be all overjoyed to have her home. I mean, I was, I just didn't *feel* overjoyed.

"We could get *you* a notebook," Suki said.

I shook my head. Writing—that wasn't my thing.

"Can I use your laptop?" I said. "I want to look up more about wolves."

Suki shut her journal and pushed it under her pillow. "We'll look them up together," she said, and we did.

It was a Friday, but Francine wasn't going out. She said there were no good bands in town, and she was only up for karaoke about once a year. Instead her three old-lady friends were coming to the house. "I've invited them for dinner," she said. "Spaghetti and garlic bread. Suki, make a salad for us, will you? Anybody you girls want to have over?"

Suki and I looked at each other. I wondered if it was too late to call Nevaeh.

Suki said, "Teena," and I grinned.

Suki called her, and I could hear her laughing on the phone. "I'd love to," she said, "but I don't know how I'd get there. Mom's got the car."

That was easy. Suki borrowed Francine's car, and the two of us went to pick up Teena.

It was already dark. We drove down the long road by the railroad tracks, across the overpass, along the road toward my old school.

Past the group home.

Suki exhaled hard when she saw it. I said, "We're never going there."

"You wouldn't have anyway," she said. "You're too young."

"You aren't there, Suki. You aren't going there. We're with Francine."

Past blocks of houses, a Baptist church, the weird vacant building with the NO TRESPASSING signs. Left-hand turn up the hill to the street where we used to live. Teena's house. Right next to Clifton's.

Clifton's house looked empty. Broken. No lights in the windows. We always kept lights on during the week—at least the kitchen light. Always. Now the dirty windows were dark and blank. The grass was raggedy and full of dead leaves. Clifton's truck wasn't parked in the drive. I wondered where it was.

Suki leaned her head against mine. We took a long slow breath together. Then someone flung open the car door, laughing. Teena jumped into the back seat. Suki peeled out of the driveway, tires squealing, and then we were all three laughing, and together like we used to be, and on our way home.

39

"The best place in the United States to see wild wolves," I said to Dr. Fremont, "is in Yellowstone National Park. That's in Wyoming, not Montana. There are actually more wolves in Montana, but they're harder to find. The ones at Yellowstone are protected, so they're not as afraid of people, and if you go to the right places early in the day you can see them."

I showed her some of the stuff Suki had helped me print out from the internet. A map of Yellowstone National Park. How it cost $700 per person to fly from East Tennessee to Yellowstone, but if you wanted to drive it would be 1,967 miles each way. "That'd take, like, three days," I said. "So it would cost a lot too. The hotel rooms at Yellowstone are super expensive but you can camp for cheap, but then you'd need a tent and stuff." I sighed. "It's all super expensive." Way more than a trip to the beach.

"The first step is to know what you want," Dr. Fremont said. "The second step is to figure out ways to get there."

I knew what I wanted, but not how to get there. That night, when Suki and I were doing the dishes after dinner, I told her I thought Yellowstone would be a safe place for us.

"Jeez, they've got, like, exploding hot springs in Yellowstone," she said. "Grizzly bears. Doesn't sound safe to me."

"Wolves," I said. "Like us." I paused. "Can't you try to testify?"

Suki shook her head. "You want two things at once," she said. "You want me to feel better enough that I can promise I'll never hurt myself again, and you want me to do something that's going to make me feel worse."

"It'll make you feel better, not worse," I said.

"If it goes well, maybe. Not if it doesn't."

I thought it would. I thought I felt better, standing up for myself at school. I'd rather get in trouble for punching Trevor than shrink away from him like Nevaeh'd done.

I'd rather fight. I said to Suki, "You're a fighter too."

Francine pulled me to one side. "I told you—knock it off. It's her choice."

I said, "She'll feel better if he stays in prison longer."

"Maybe. But it'd be the hardest thing she'd ever have

to do, Della. Harder than taking care of you when she was eight years old. Your sister just got out of the hospital. I don't know how much she can take."

"She's a wolf," I said.

Francine said, "You're carrying this wolf thing a little far. She's a wolf to *you*. She may not feel like one herself. Leave her be."

40

Next day, Suki came home with a tattoo.

It was on the same wrist she cut, right beside her scar. It was a semicolon, a piece of punctuation that looks like this: ;

"You use semicolons when you don't want to use a period," Suki said. Her eyes were sparkling. "This is to remind myself. My sentence—my story—it's going to keep going on."

Okay, that was cool.

"You wanted me to do more," she said. "To make promises. Here it is. The best promise I can make right now. Anytime I look at my wrist, I won't just see what I almost did. I'll see what I'm going to do—keep going."

I looked at my own smooth wrist, the veins running either side of the tendons in the center. The artery Suki cut ran deeper. It connected directly to Suki's heart. I said, "I want one too."

She frowned. "Um, no. You're ten. Also you didn't— This is a special sort of symbol, Della. You can't wear it. People will think something about you that isn't true."

"But it is true," I said. "My story is still going on."

"Yep," Suki said. "Not the same."

Francine didn't care at all that Suki'd gotten a tattoo, without permission, even though she's underage. "Think I asked permission for any of my tats?" she said. "It's your skin, sugar, do what you want."

I said, "Why are you so relaxed about everything?" She was taking up a whole bunch of her time hauling us to our appointments and things, not to mention gas money, not to mention that going to the Y cost money, and she kept acting like it was all no big deal. "Why are you so helpful?"

Francine said, "I wished someone had helped me when I was Suki's age. Or yours." She blew out a cloud of cigarette smoke. "Wish I'd had someone on my side."

Oh.

Snow, it was such a hard world.

"You said you only keep foster kids for the money," I reminded her.

She shrugged. "I couldn't do it if they didn't pay me. Couldn't afford to. But I didn't say 'only,' did I?"

I thought she did. Maybe I was wrong.

Later that week, our social worker came back. She talked about Suki's return to school and about our therapy appointments, and then she brought up the Permanency Plan.

Suki surprised me. "I was thinking something in the medical field," she said.

"You mean a *doctor*?" I said.

"No," she said. "They had all sorts of people doing different jobs at the hospital. At both hospitals. Drawing blood and running tests. Taking X-rays. Stuff like that."

The social worker nodded excitedly. "Medical technicians," she said. "That'd be a great goal. The high school has some health sciences class that would get you started."

"I know," Suki said. "My guidance counselor said I could take one next semester."

The social worker wrote a few things down. "You'd need to graduate high school and then take one or two more years of classes. So you might stay—"

Suki held up her hand. "I don't know. I'm not saying that yet." She sighed. "It's not easy, missing three weeks of school and coming back with this scar on my wrist."

I said, "And a semicolon."

She smiled at me. "Which is part of why I got the semicolon, right? But"—Suki looked at the social worker—"I'm not saying anything yet. Just maybe."

That *maybe* was more than we ever had before.

"How about you, Della?"

"I want to go to Yellowstone National Park."

The social worker blinked. "When?"

"Soon as I can." I pointed to her notebook. "Write it down. Yellowstone. National. Park."

"But that's in Wyoming—"

Which was farther away than Kansas. "Yes."

Then it was Friday again. Suki'd worked a short shift midweek, then begged to be put back on Friday night. "You know what I love?" she said when we were driving there in the car. We'd dropped Francine off at O'Maillin's. "When I'm scanning groceries really fast, and the register goes *bing-bing-bing-bing-bing*. It's like music, you know? Or winning the lottery."

I did not know, but I loved seeing her smile.

Coach Tony was standing near the front door, wearing his official Food City shirt and a pair of khaki pants. "Hey Coach!" I said.

"Hey, sunshine!" he said. To Suki he said, "Welcome back."

"Thanks," said Suki.

"Della tell you about the Y's rec basketball league?" he asked her. "I want her to sign up for it so she gets some playing experience before middle school. I'm the coach for the middle school teams."

Suki raised her eyebrows. "That sounds fun."

I shook my head. "Forty bucks," I said. I'd asked.

"Oh."

"We have some scholarships available," Coach Tony said. "You'd have to come early, help get the gym set up. Sweep the floors, that kind of thing."

"Really?" I could do that. Maybe Nevaeh could do it with me.

Suki went to the office to check in. I ran to the deli. Maybelline handed me a cookie the minute she saw me. Chocolate chip. I broke it into two pieces and handed half back. "We'll share," I said. "I'll do the saltshakers tonight too."

She bit into the cookie. "That's good," she said. "I missed you. How are you? How's your sister?"

I looked up at Maybelline. "I think she's better. I'm scared she's not, but I think she is. She just got a semicolon tattooed on her wrist. Did you know tattoos never ever go away?"

"Well, sure," Maybelline said. "That's why I never got one. I change my mind more often than some people change their underwear."

I wandered around the store and checked out the creamer selection. (New flavor: classic cinnamon roll.) I wiped down the deli tables and filled up all the salt. Pepper too, though folks don't use nearly as much pepper. I straightened up some of the fruit displays. Round ten o'clock I started doing the grocery shopping and that's when I found the most amazing thing. There's a teeny section of books at Food City, in the aisle with the greeting cards and pencils and baby supplies. Most of the books have half-naked cowboys or swooning long-haired white women on the cover, but there were usually a couple of kids' books too, Sesame Street and Disney princesses, and sometimes cookbooks or books about gardening or trucks, down on the bottom row.

None of that would interest me even if I liked books, but somehow, as I was rolling the cart past, I happened to look down at that bottom row, and there was a coloring book about wolves.

Honest. Wolves. It wasn't a baby coloring book, either—it was some kind of fancy one, and the wolves were swirly and intricate and fierce.

I'd never fallen in love with a coloring book before. I'd never even owned one, that I knew of. I dropped to my knees and grabbed this one—it was crazy, it was the only one in the rack, like it had been put there just for me. It cost ten bucks, but I didn't care. I took it over to Suki. "If my part of the ten percent isn't enough, I'll pay you back, I swear," I said. She waved me off and fetched her good markers out of her purse.

I sat in the deli the rest of the night. I colored one wolf

in reds and browns and golds, and gave it to Maybelline, who hung it up behind the deli counter. I colored one in greens and yellows for Tony, and one in blues and black and purple for Suki. Then I did one in a whole rainbow of colors, and that one was for me.

41

So everything felt super until Monday morning, when I went and asked Suki another question. I don't fault myself for asking. I mean, I needed to know. The alarm clock had just gone off, and we were lying still half-asleep. I said, "How many times did he hurt you?

She shrugged. "It probably wasn't every week."

It took a moment for this to sink in. I sat up. "Almost every week? For *years*?"

Whenever Suki felt really sad her eyes got bigger. Right now they looked like they might swallow her whole face. "Years," she said. "The whole time."

Dr. Fremont and Francine both say Suki and I have to

live in the present. I get that, but the past keeps sneaking up on us and walloping us upside our heads.

When I got to school I was not in the best place to be dealing with snow from Trevor. Maybe he guessed that. Maybe he saw it as some kind of challenge. Right after breakfast he accidentally-on-purpose bumped into me in the hallway. I accidentally-on-purpose bumped him back. Hard.

At recess he pinched Luisa while she was talking to me. "Stop it!" Luisa yelled, but he was already laughing and running away.

The whistle blew. Recess was over. I sat down at my desk. Honestly, I'd had about all the snow I could take.

I turned around and glared at Trevor. He smirked back. Ms. Davonte said, "Della, turn around." I did, but not before I saw Trevor lean over and whisper something to the boy who sat next to him. They both looked at me and laughed. I didn't do anything. Couldn't, with Ms. Davonte up at the whiteboard giving me the stink eye.

We had math class. At the end of it, Ms. Davonte gave us time to do a worksheet. I was bent over, working on it, entirely for once minding my own business. I wasn't even thinking about Trevor anymore. But when he got up to take his paper to the podium at the front, on his way past me, he reached down and grabbed the skin of my back. Hard.

I jumped to my feet. I spun around and stepped forward so my entire body was about an inch away from Trevor's. I pulled my fist back to punch him.

And then I didn't.

I didn't punch him.

Instead I looked him straight in the eye. I said, loud and clear into the silence that had fallen on the class, "You just pinched me, and you need to stop. Never touch me again. Never touch me or any girl in this class without permission *ever again*."

Trevor took a step back. He almost looked scared. I was taller than he was. Heavier too. And about twenty times more fierce.

I was a wolf.

"Della!" Ms. Davonte said. She came up between us. "Della, sit down!"

I said, "I will not. Not until he promises to stop grabbing me."

"I didn't touch her," Trevor said.

"Did too!" I said.

"Really, Ms. Davonte"—Trevor looked up, his face all innocent—"I didn't."

"You stupid—"

I didn't say the next word. (Snowman.) Instead I looked at Ms. Davonte. "Check my back," I said.

"What?"

"Look down the back of my shirt," I said. "You'll see a mark where he pinched me."

Evidence.

"Della, don't be ridiculous," Ms. Davonte said. She sounded super annoyed. A fight between her two least-favorite students. She didn't want to believe either one of us.

I looked over my shoulder. Found Nevaeh. Looked straight at her.

Her eyes asked, *Do you want help?*

Mine answered, *Yes. Please.*

Nevaeh got to her feet. "Trevor's lying," she said. "I saw him pinch Della. Also, he does it to me too."

Across the room, Luisa stood up. She looked scared but she did it. She said, "At recess today he pinched my back."

"Pinched your back?" Ms. Davonte asked.

Luisa said, "He thinks it's funny we don't wear bras."

Mackinleigh stood up. "He does that to me too."

Another girl stood. And another. And one more. Six girls standing, besides me. Trevor's face went red.

"He does it all the time," Nevaeh said, loud and clear. "He does it, and he laughs at us."

Mackinleigh said, "I started wearing my sister's old bras and he still does it. He snaps the strap. I told him not to and he doesn't care."

Luisa said, very softly, "It hurts. I told him to stop."

"I've told him three times," I said. "He does not have permission to touch me."

Ms. Davonte looked stunned. Like she'd jumped into an ice-cold swimming pool. "Trevor," Ms. Davonte said, "go to the office and have a seat. I'll be with you in a minute."

Trevor slouched out. The rest of the class sat very still. Even Trevor's friends weren't laughing. We'd never seen this kind of look on Ms. Davonte's face before. She studied us, turned her head and looked at every single person, especially the girls who were standing. "How long has this been going on?" she asked.

Nobody said anything.

"Why didn't any of you say something?" Ms. Davonte said. "Della's right. No one is allowed to touch anyone else without permission. We had a whole conversation about this at the start of the year."

Nevaeh said, "I told my teacher last year. Trevor said he didn't do it. The teacher thought I was lying."

Luisa said, "My dad says I have to fight my own battles. But I don't like fighting."

I said, "You think you already know all the answers about me. You don't listen."

Ms. Davonte sighed. "I'm sorry," she said. She looked sorry. "Clearly this is something I should have been aware of. Girls, sit down—but thank you for standing up and speaking out." She looked back at me. "Della," she said, "you get on down to the office too."

42

Dr. Penny and Ms. Davonte called Francine and told her to take time off work and come to the school. "Why?" I argued. "Trevor started it. It wasn't my fault."

"You aren't in trouble," Dr. Penny said, "but you need a parent or guardian here for this."

"Why?" I got up and paced around the office. Trevor just sat, looking at his shoes. "Francine'll have to take emergency vacation time. She won't be happy."

Dr. Penny said, "I imagine she won't," like that was not a big deal at all. "She's your foster parent. This is a situation that calls for your parent to be here."

■ ■ ■

We sat in that office for almost an hour, waiting. My stomach tied itself in knots. Trevor stretched out his legs and spread his arms, like he was just relaxing, not worried at all, but I noticed how fast and shallow he was breathing.

Part of me wanted to tell him to take a big deep breath. Let it out slow.

Part of me did not.

The longer we sat there, the more nervous Trevor looked. I wondered what his story was. Wondered how many bad things had happened to him.

No matter how many it was, it didn't make it okay for him to harass me.

Trevor's mom showed up wearing a uniform from a fast-food place. She gave both Trevor and me the same kind of glare. Didn't say anything. Francine strolled in right after her, all unhurried, like this was just a normal part of her day. Before anybody could say much, Dr. Penny had us all move into a room where we could sit around a big table. Ms. Davonte came back. She told Trevor's mom and Francine what she saw, and what I said, and Nevaeh, and Mackinleigh, and Luisa. And how the other girls stood up too.

Trevor's mom had a hard, mean face. She said she didn't understand the fuss about a little teasing, and also if anyone was a bully it was me. I'd punched him, hadn't I?

"That was last week," I said, "not today. But I'd do it again—"

"Della," Francine said, "shut up." Her face got as hard as Trevor's mother's and her expression more pug dog than ever. She started talking, long stern sentences with words like *harassment* and *safe learning environment*. It took me a while to realize she was actually on my side.

"I want to see the school handbook," Francine said. "Let's look up what each of these students has actually done."

Come to find out "inappropriate touching" was a *thing*. First offense: *three days'* in-school suspension. Which meant Trevor would have to do worksheets in the library, by himself, for three whole days.

"This wasn't the first time," I said.

The principal gave Ms. Davonte a sideways kind of look. "I understand," she said, "but this is the first documented time."

"There were seven of us," I said. "Seven offenses."

"Yes." The principal seemed to be considering.

"That's ridiculous!" Trevor's mom spat. She started to talk about how her son Daniel had been targeted too, how teachers at this school had it in for her boys. Her voice rose high and angry. She turned to Trevor. "I can't believe you're letting a girl get the better of you."

"Right," Francine said, picking up the handbook again. "So what did Della do?"

What I'd done, at least this time, was pretty much nothing. I had disrupted class. I hadn't hit anybody, or damaged anything, or, for once, used any bad words. "Disrupting class" gave you a Reflection Recess, which meant *sit and think about what you've done*. Which I had pretty much done for an hour already.

Trevor looked shocked. Like, he never thought anything he was doing was a big deal.

"I wish the girls had come to me earlier," Ms. Davonte said. "I wish I'd been paying better attention."

I said, "It's hard to talk about hard things. Especially to people that don't listen."

Ms. Davonte looked at me. "Right," she said. "I understand."

"Trevor," Dr. Penny said, "what do you have to say?"

He looked up, and he looked sideways at his mom, and he flinched a little. I knew he was afraid. A mean part of me wanted to feel glad—let him be afraid, for once—but most of me wasn't. I didn't think Trevor was evil, like Clifton. Not really. I knew I didn't know his story.

I wondered who Trevor was afraid of, and why.

"Daniel started it," he said. "Snapping bra straps. You know, for fun. But the girls in fourth grade mostly don't wear bras, so, you know . . ." His voice trailed off.

Ms. Davonte said, "How is that fun?"

Trevor's mother said, "It's just teasing. All boys—"

"You know," Trevor said. "It's funny. It makes the other boys laugh." He shifted uncomfortably.

I remembered, back at my old school, how I tried to

make people laugh. Because I wanted to have a friend. Because I wanted people to like me. Trevor was the only kid with his name on the whiteboard.

I said, "The girls never thought it was funny. I hate it."

"Some girls like it," he said.

"I bet not. How would you like it if all the girls started grabbing the front of your pants?"

Trevor's mom said, "Oh, that's not—"

Francine said, "It's exactly the same."

Trevor didn't say anything, but his eyes got big.

"Didn't think so," I said. "So knock it off."

Trevor looked at me for half a second, then dropped his gaze. "Okay," he said. "I'm, you know. I'm sorry."

Trevor's mom started on about how this was Not Fair and making too much of a little thing, and boys would be boys, everybody expected that, it wasn't like you'd want them to be sissies. The principal said there was nothing boyish about bad behavior and made her sign some paper about the in-school suspension.

"What's *she* going to get?" Trevor's mom said, pointing at me.

Dr. Penny said I would be disciplined appropriately. She excused Trevor's mom, and Trevor. After they left, Dr. Penny turned to me. "If he does touch you inappropriately again, him or anyone else, I want to hear about it right away. Okay?"

I nodded.

Dr. Penny said, "I'm proud of you for using words this

time. *Appropriate* words. That shows progress, Della. Go on back to class."

Francine said, "I think I'll just take her home."

"You don't have to," I said, fast. "I'll behave."

"Nah. Enough's enough."

Francine waited for me to get my backpack. We got in the car. She drove straight to McDonald's.

Seriously. She bought us each a chocolate milkshake.

"I'm not trying to mess things up," I said, sucking hard on my straw.

"You didn't mess nothing up," she said, sucking hard on hers. "You did good."

43

At home, Suki said, "Huh. He got in trouble, and you didn't?"

"That's right," I said. "I didn't even say *snow*."

"Huh," said Suki. "That's awesome. Good for you."

Next morning was my appointment with Dr. Fremont. When she handed me a feelings paper, I circled *annoyed* but not *angry*. *Worried* but not *scared*. *Strong*, not *invisible*. I circled *resilient*. I circled *proud*.

Dr. Fremont looked at the paper. "That's a nice improvement," she said.

Then she took out the little workbook that we did sometimes when I was there. "I think it's time for you to start writing down your story," she said. She showed me pages where I was supposed to write down what happened to me, and how I felt about it, and also what I wanted to happen next. My future story. My Permanency Plan.

The workbook left two and a half pages blank for me to write my story. I shook my head. "I'm going to need a lot more paper than that."

At school I got to class early. I reached into my desk and pulled out the creamer Nevaeh and I traded back and forth.

Southern butter pecan. I swear, someday I was going to try it. It couldn't be worse than fat-free full-sugar French vanilla. I walked over and placed it on Nevaeh's desk.

Nevaeh came in, saw the creamer, and smiled.

"You're my hero," I said.

She looked around. "Where's Trevor?"

"Library. Three-day suspension."

She said, "I can't believe it."

I said, "Even Ms. Davonte couldn't ignore all of us." We'd worked as a pack, all us girls. A wolf pack.

"I guess not," Nevaeh said.

At recess, Luisa came up and thanked me. Mackinleigh shook her head. "I'm worried," she said. "Now he'll just do it when the teachers aren't around."

I said, "Not if we all work together. Not if we make sure he knows that every one of us will tell on him anytime he does. Second offense for inappropriate touching is out-of-school suspension." That meant he'd have to stay home with his angry mother for at least three days. I didn't think he'd risk it. Picking on us wasn't that much fun.

Second offense for punching someone was also out-of-school suspension. If I had actually punched Trevor a second time, instead of speaking up, I'd be sitting at home now. Pretty sure Francine wouldn't have bought me a milkshake.

"I'm not going to hit him again," I said.

Nevaeh grinned at me. "You gonna quit cussing?"

I grinned back. "Probably not," I said. "I like strong words."

We ran over to the swing set and had a contest to see who could swing the highest. I was trying my best but I didn't have a chance. Luisa was a swing set ninja.

I was soaring in the air, thinking about Trevor, and Clifton, and Suki. And thinking about my new pack.

All at once, I knew what I needed to do. I stopped swinging. I took a deep breath. It was the best possible thing, if I was brave enough to do it.

I was.

44

At dinner I said, "I need to talk to my lawyer." We were having spaghetti again. Not as good as mac 'n' cheese, but close.

Francine choked on her can of soda. "What for? You planning to sue somebody?"

"I've got a lawyer, I ought to be able to talk to him." I'd met him. Not for very long, and not lately, but he said not to expect to see him much until closer to the trial.

"Of course," Francine said. "But—"

Suki's eyes went wolf-like. Wary. She put her fork down and stared at me. "Why do you need to talk to the lawyer, Della?"

I stared right back. "Because I am going to testify

against Clifton in person. I don't want to use that video."

"Why not?" said Suki. "The video will work just as well. You've already made it. You don't need to talk about all that stuff again."

"I want to," I said. "I'm going to sit in that courtroom in front of everyone."

"It will be super hard," Suki said. "In front of everyone. In front of Clifton."

"In front of Clifton," I agreed. "I'm going to tell everyone exactly what he did to me. And then"—I paused here, took a big breath, kept going—"I'm going to tell them every-thing I can about what he did to you."

Francine whistled between her teeth.

Suki went pale. "No, you aren't," she said.

"Yes. I am."

Suki said, "It's my story."

I said, "It's your story and it's mine. I don't know how you feel. I can't tell them exactly what he did to you, or when. But everything he did to you hurt me too. It's as much my story to tell as it is yours. I'm going to tell them everything I know about both of us."

Suki rested her forehead in her hands. She said, "You don't have any idea how difficult that will be."

I said, "I do. I'm doing it anyway."

Suki said, "Della, think about it. Really think. You want to talk out loud, in person, in a courtroom? They'll be trying to find holes in your story. They'll be trying to prove you're a liar."

"I won't be lying," I said, "so they won't be able to."

She said, "You don't know the details. Not what he did to me."

"I'll tell them everything I do know," I said. "I'll ask Teena to tell them too. She'll do it, for us."

Suki and I stared at each other. I said, "I do know how hard it will be. I'm still going to do it."

"Francine," Suki said, "tell her it's a bad idea."

Francine slurped up spaghetti and shrugged. "If she's that brave, I ain't gonna stop her."

Suki got up. She put her plate in the sink and went into the bathroom. I felt a fluttering of fear in my gut. Any knives in the bathroom? Any medicines or poisons or other harmful stuff in there?

The toilet flushed and Suki came out. She sat back down at the table. "Don't look so panicky, Della," she said. She flashed her wrist at me. The semicolon tattoo. "I promised, didn't I?" She looked hard at me for another moment. "It really scared you, didn't it? Just my going to the bathroom."

"Yep," I said.

She grimaced. "I'm so sorry. What I did scared you so bad."

We did the dishes and then Suki opened her laptop and spread her homework across the kitchen table. I got out my coloring book and started working on a female wolf, strong and beautiful, howling at the moon.

"Della," Suki said, after a while.

I looked up.

"Come look at this video I found."

I scooched my chair around until I could see the screen. Suki hit play.

It was about the wolves in Yellowstone.

It started with a picture of a white wolf howling. A man's voice began to tell the story.

Wolves had been extinct at Yellowstone for a long time. Over seventy years. Then, in 1995, some people moved a small pack back into the park. Fourteen wolves.

At the time, there were too many deer in the park. They were eating all the plants and causing lots of damage. The wolves ate some of the deer, and scared others away. The grass started to grow back, and then the trees. Beavers came back. Foxes and rabbits and mice came back. Weasels and hawks and songbirds and eagles. The riverbanks quit eroding. The rivers grew deeper and more stable.

The wolves made everything better.

When we finished watching, Suki looked at me. She said, "It wasn't very many wolves, but they changed everything."

I nodded. She clicked a few keys. "Here's something else I found. The Yellowstone Youth Conservation Corps." The pictures showed a bunch of kids Suki's age, wearing yellow hard hats and tan shirts. "It's for high school students," she said. "They work for a month at Yellowstone."

"They get paid?" I said. "It's like a real job?"

Suki nodded. "And they give you food and housing."

"Shoo," I said. I almost couldn't imagine it. Getting paid to live among the wolves.

Suki flipped back to the video and started it again. On the screen, the white wolf pointed her nose to the sky and howled. It was the most beautiful sound.

"Do you think I could—I mean we could—"

"If I get a car," Suki said, "we could drive out there."

I said, "Could we stop and see Mama on the way?"

Suki stared at the wolves. "Not a good idea, Della," she said. "It won't help. Mama won't ever be the way we need her to be."

"I still want to see her," I said.

"She won't be good."

"I just want a memory that isn't that motel room."

Suki gave me a hug. "Okay. We can try."

She started the video a third time. Wolves at Yellowstone. I could see it starting to fall into place. A real Permanency Plan. "Suki," I said, "it's great to be a wolf."

She looked up at me but didn't say anything.

"Do you mind my telling your story? In court?" I asked.

She took a deep breath. Held it, blew it out. "Yes," she said. "But Francine's right. It's your story too. I can't stop you."

"Will you be angry with me?"

"I don't think so. Not if I can help it."

"I looked it up," I said. "If I tell them everything Clifton did, he might get twenty years."

"Only if they believe you," Suki said. "They probably won't."

I said, "I want to try."

45

I went to sleep happy with my decision. *I* would be the strong sister, for a change. I would speak out. I would help Suki.

She wouldn't have to sit in court with Clifton scowling at her. She wouldn't have to feel so afraid.

I went to sleep, but something was bothering me around the edges of my mind. When I woke up I knew what it was.

The alarm clock hadn't gone off yet, but it was starting to get light outside. Well past Suki's screaming hour. She hadn't had a nightmare since she came home.

She was sleeping hard now, on her back, softly snoring. I nudged her. "Wake up."

Her eyes fluttered open. "What?"

"I figured something out," I said. "You're wrong about having to testify in person. You can do it on tape. Remember?"

"I'll have to answer questions if I want anyone to believe me. In person. With him there."

"You won't," I said. "They can ask your doctors questions. Your therapists. Everyone you told in the hospital. You can just talk on the tape. Like you already did."

Tears swam up in her eyes. She said, "Only children get to testify on tape."

"Suki," I said. My breath caught in my throat. "You were a child."

She stared at me. "You *are* a child," I said. "A kid. You still are."

She shook her head. "I never got to be a kid. Somebody had to be the grown-up." Tears filled her lower eyelids, threatening to overflow.

"You had to act like a grown-up," I said. "You weren't one. You were just a little kid." I could feel my own eyes filling. "You were so little, Suki. You did your best, but even now—you're not a grown-up. You're a girl."

We'd needed a mama to protect us. Or a father. Or both. We'd needed our own pack of wolves, to watch over us until we were grown.

Tears poured down Suki's face. "Sometimes," she whispered, "I feel so sorry for that scared little girl."

Tears rolled down my cheeks too. I nodded. "Me too," I said. "I still do."

Suki put her face into her pillow. Her shoulders shook. She sobbed and sobbed and sobbed and sobbed. I lay down next to her, my head against hers, holding her tight.

Eventually we both quit crying. Suki's breath came easier. She didn't say anything, but she didn't have to. I already knew what she would do.

46

The next night, Suki worked a short shift at Food City. At home I messed around on her laptop. I was looking up two things. The first was Suki's semicolon.

It was a symbol of survival. Of hope.

I was a survivor too, but not in quite the same way as Suki. I started looking for my second thing. Eventually I found it.

I went into the living room and plopped down beside Francine. She was playing a game on her phone and watching TV. "Yo," she said.

"Yo," I said. "You know how you gotta pay for everything Suki and me absolutely need?"

She hit pause on her game and looked up. "Yeah," she

said. "You're probably right, and I know your sister can't afford it yet. I'll get you a phone. Just don't expect it to go on the internet."

"Not that." I showed her a piece of paper.

"What?" she said. "It's an 'and' symbol, right?"

"Yeah," I said. "It's called an ampersand. It also means union. Or going on a journey. Or"—I'd written this down because I liked it so much but knew I'd never remember it exactly. I read it out—"*an expectation for something more to occur.*"

Francine said, "That little squiggly thing?"

I said, "When it's a tattoo."

Francine stared at me. "Oh snow," she said. "I'd be contributing to the delinquency of a minor."

"Suki's a minor."

"Not nearly as much as you."

"I won't tell anybody."

"I think it would be a very bad idea."

"Francine?"

"Tattoos hurt like snow, you know. Also they're permanent."

"Right," I said. "This is another part of my Permanency Plan."

Francine looked at me without blinking for practically a minute. Then she went back to her phone. "I'm getting you some kind of big cuff bracelet," she said. "Big enough to cover it. I want you to wear it every single time your caseworker is anywhere around."

I nodded, grinning.

"Or in court," she said.

"Absolutely in court," I said.

Francine sniffed. "I'll have to call my buddy. See if he'll bring some stuff by the house. Nobody's going to tattoo a ten-year-old in broad daylight in a store. That's way too illegal."

I grinned so hard, my cheeks started hurting. "Thanks, Francine."

"Yeah, whatever. I suppose you want one for Suki too?"

"That's the idea."

When Suki came home I showed her the ampersand. She said, "You're the smartest, best sister in the whole wide world."

47

So Francine's buddy, who was tattooed pretty much everywhere except the palms of his hands, came and inked two perfect ampersands, one on Suki's wrist—across the scar from the semicolon—and the other on mine. He didn't even charge Francine. "Public service," he said. "My good deed for the year."

And here I am at school, just come back from recess, Ms. Davonte staring at my wrist. "Della," she says, "is that a real tattoo?"

"Yes, ma'am," I say, holding it up.

An expectation for something more to occur.

Suki's going to testify on tape. I am going to testify in person. I want to. I know it will be hard, but Suki promises she'll sit somewhere I can see her. I'll look at my sister's face instead of Clifton's. If I need to, I can look down at my wrist and see the same symbol that's on Suki's. She can do that too. Our stories will be separate but always intertwined.

Standing just inside the fourth-grade classroom, I look up at Ms. Davonte. I smile. I say, "This is to remind me of the best day of my life."

She looks down at me. For a wonder, she smiles back. "When was that?" she asks.

"Tomorrow," I say.

And that right there, that's the very best part of this story.

AUTHOR'S NOTE

The first thing I want you to know is, it happened to me.

The second thing is, I was able to heal. It took time, and work, and I did it. People can always heal.

When I was a child I was sexually abused. It was hard and bad and affected my life in lots of difficult ways. I didn't tell anyone for a very long time. When I started being able to talk about it, other people began telling me their stories too. Lots of them. I realized that a lot of people are affected by sexual abuse. Most of them find it very hard to talk about, but being able to talk about it is one of the first steps toward overcoming the damage it caused.

Eventually I found my words. I wrote this book hoping it would help readers find theirs.

Why is it so hard to talk about? I think it's because children who are assaulted are forced to deal with adult stuff years before they're ready to. They don't understand what happened to them. They're powerless, and frightened. They imagine there must be something wrong with them—that somehow, what happened must be their fault. (It never is.)

Some families face struggles like addiction and mental health disorders that make everything worse. When adults can't take proper care of children, the children—like Suki—end up having to act like adults themselves, taking on responsibilities they aren't ready to handle. It's difficult, and damaging, to have to be an adult when you aren't finished being a child.

Families can look healthy on the surface but still be entirely messed up. You can't always tell by looking at someone whether or not they're having a hard time.

So what do we do? Start by believing. If someone tells you they've been hurt, or they need help, believe them. Say, "I'm really sorry." Say, "It's not your fault." Say, "You're very brave to speak up. I'm proud of you."

If you're the person who was hurt, start by believing it wasn't your fault. Believe, too, that it was wrong, and harmful, and that you deserve help. Work on finding your words.

As soon as you can, get help—for yourself or for the friend who trusted you. Tell your parents if you can, or any other adult you trust. If that person doesn't help you, tell someone else. Teachers, police officers, and doctors are all mandatory reporters. That means when someone tells them about sexual abuse, they are required to make an official report. Tell any adult that you trust, and keep telling them, until they help you.

One of the things Della learns about in this book is consent. Consent is actually pretty easy: It means that nobody can do things to your body without your permission—and permission means saying yes, not just not saying no. Sometimes we aren't used to asking for consent, to saying "Hey, would you like a hug?" when our friends look sad. It's good to get used to asking for consent. Practice it. And always listen when someone tells you no.

Kids actually can't give consent to certain adult things. They're too young. In some cases it doesn't matter at all whether or not a child would be willing to give consent—they simply can't. The kid is never to blame in these situations. The adult always is.

No matter how bad something in your life makes you feel, know that bad feelings are temporary. People can always heal. We can always get better. I promise.

If you're looking for more information on how to get help or to help someone, I recommend the websites seekthenspeak.org and startbybelieving.org. You can also contact RAINN (Rape, Abuse & Incest National Network), the nation's largest anti–sexual violence organization, at rainn.org or 800-656-HOPE. If you want to know more statistics about sexual abuse and children, you can find some on my website, www.kimberlybrubakerbradley.com.

Finally, if you've ever thought about hurting yourself, please, please don't. Lots of places will help you. You can call the National Suicide Prevention Lifeline twenty-four hours a day—suicidepreventionlifeline.org or 800-273-8255.

Last of all, be a wolf. Take care of your pack. And fight.

If you want to think more about the topics covered in this book, here are some questions you could go over with your friends. (Thanks to Room 228 Educational Consulting for their help compiling them.)

1. Why does Della say Suki's superpower is to make herself invisible? How does it help Suki to be invisible? What might happen if people really saw her?

2. Are people in Della's life really seeing her? She's not invisible, but she's good at putting up a mask to hide behind. Is this good or bad? How does it help or hurt her?

3. How does Ms. Davonte see Della? Dr. Penny? Francine? Which comes closest to seeing the real Della?

4. How does Della learn to show herself? What helps her find her words? What helps her keep fighting?

5. How does Della's love for Suki change the story? How does Suki's love for Della? How does having someone who loves us help us be honest and strong?

6. The scariest moment of the book is when Suki hurts herself. Why is this the worst thing she could do? Why won't Suki promise Della that she'll never do it again? Should she be able to make that kind of promise?

7. Why is Della's story so hard to tell? What makes her brave enough to tell it?

ACKNOWLEDGMENTS

This was not an easy book to write, and there were times, while writing it, when I was not an easy person to be around. Thanks to everyone who hung in with me. Thanks to the many people who gave me shelter and support.

Christa Desir read a very early draft and provided valuable feedback. Shauna Nefos Webb, PhD, read a later draft for authenticity, and Dr. Jennifer Hartstein did the same at the end. Thank you all very much for your expertise. These are complex topics; while I've tried hard to make Della and Suki's experiences real and true, they aren't universal. Your healing may come about differently.

My mom and dad are my favorite copyeditors (though errors remaining are my own). I love my siblings and I'm grateful they love this book. My merry band of nephews gives us joy and inspiration.

Dial Books for Young Readers, Lauri Hornik, and Jessica Dandino Garrison: Right from the first thirty-nine-page unpunctuated stream-of-consciousness, exceedingly rough draft, Della's story mattered more to me than anything else I've ever written. You not only allowed but enthusiastically encouraged me to craft a novel for ten-year-olds featuring sexual assault, a suicide attempt, foster care, homelessness, meth addiction, and eighty-six uses of the word snow. Your support has meant and always will mean the world to me. I hope you like me, you're stuck with me now.

My children fill my life with laughter, love, sarcasm, snark, and regular reminders of how very lucky I am. My husband, Bart Bradley, is the bravest man I ever met. He knows how much I owe him. I hope he knows how much I love him too.

For several years, survivors of sexual assault have been entrusting me with their stories. Thank you, all of you, for your courage and tenacity. I hope you feel I listened. I've found my words. I pray that someday you will too.

KIMBERLY BRUBAKER BRADLEY

is the author of several middle grade novels, including the widely acclaimed *Jefferson's Sons* and the *New York Times* bestsellers *The War I Finally Won* and *The War That Saved My Life*, which also earned a Newbery Honor and a Schneider Award. She and her husband have two grown children and live with their dog, several ponies, a highly opinionated mare, and a surplus of cats on a fifty-two acre farm in Bristol, Tennessee. Learn more about Kim on her website, kimberlybrubakerbradley.com and her blog, kimberly-brubaker-bradley.blogspot.com, and connect with her on Twitter @kimbbbradley and on Facebook at kimberly.b.bradley.5.

&